CORRUPTED AMBITION

by Obi Orakwue

CORRUPTED AMBITION

by Obi Orakwue

Obrake Books

OBRAKE CANADA INC.
TORONTO, ONTARIO

Book designed by Leigh Beadon.

Library and Archives Canada Cataloguing in Publication

Orakwue, Obi
     Corrupted ambition / Obi Orakwue.

ISBN 978-0-9782703-1-5

    I. Title.

PS8629.R35C67 2007   C813'.6   C2007-900809-7

Printed in Canada by Webcom Inc., Toronto, ON

**First Published in Canada in 2007
by Obrake Books.**
Obrake Canada Inc.
Toronto, Ontario Canada.
www.obrake.com/books

This work is dedicated to my dearest friends: Echezona Santiago, Chinedu, Phillip, Victor and Obieze. I love you all.

Ambition indeed always is good
But like in love with abundance
When you're never satisfied with increase
Real ambition never relents
I'd wondered severally
What corrupts like ambition
Power I guess
But the tortuous route to power
Gilded and empowered by ambition
Ambition really corrupts!

— BY OBI ORAKWUE

CHAPTER 1
West London
July 1999

Bradley noticed the receding interest and an awakening sign of puzzle on Tom's face, as Tom adjusted himself in his seat, ran a hand through his kinky hair, and moved his head in an arc, his glance cutting across the lounge. The atmosphere was normal on that classic summer afternoon in Europe's most horizontal and conservative capital city, London, in the Lounge Bar of the Hilton Hotels Limited. Phrases like bullish stocks, short selling, and share prices were thrown around as casually as Londoners discuss social security and Euro-integration. Ladies with expensive hair styles, enhanced cheekbones and fuller lips than ever, wearing lipstick colours that are truly permanent and could only be removed by laser and varnish, teetering on adorable shoes with curving heels, brandishing expensive gilded leather handbags from which they pull ostrich and fish skin wallets to tip the waiters. Harassed looking executives on tea break streamed in and out of the lounge, bidding acquaintances and colleagues wooden byes and hellos. Waiters of normal formality garbed in identical white gabardine suits and red bow ties wheel tea carts across the lounge serving tea, coffee and cakes. The lounge manager in an assumed sunny mood, beaming and making wise cracks, playing the cheerful host, slowly paced the aisles inspecting the quality of service in the lounge, occasionally admonishing the waiters to improve their services by a mere harsh gaze. In the floor above, camera flashes exploded furiously where an opera star was holding court.

"Don't worry, it will all work out fine. You must remember that the route to abundance and the ensuing real freedom is often tortuous. We've got fifty-fifty risk-benefit ratio to shoulder. I've got the formula, the intellectual capital and responsibility. Hard earned intellectual capital," said Bradley.

"How hard earned?" Tom asked.

"Well, not too hard though, but not as easy and lucky a strike as out-living a generous creditor," Bradley replied.

Tom didn't like the insinuation, but he said nothing and betrayed no emotion, he merely looked up from his cup of tea and gazed vacantly into Bradley's face. He hadn't expected so many niceties for the day. It would actually be an extravagant expectation for a day he woke up with a humiliating experience. He had made and honoured the appointment to escape the ominous boredom of the day, a triple barrelled ominous day - the twentieth of July. Besides, he's learnt never to be crabby since laying his sweaty palms on whopping £20 million cash, banked some and invested the rest. And for all intent and purpose is ready to spend his last pint of energy to multiply it enough to make the question: "what shall I do with all this money and fortune?" worth asking, rather than getting stressed by low budget men like Bradley. He knows that critics like Bradley, who points out how the strong stumbled and why the winner won, don't count. It's men like himself who know the great enthusiasm, the great devotions, and euphoria of high achievement, who only fail while daring valiantly, that count.

He gazed back at Bradley, and listened as he continued his briefing.

"It is listed among diseases classified as 'orphan diseases'," said Bradley. "It is suffered by very few people
and have no drugs for cure in the market, the few people who have been treated of the disease were treated
with experimental drugs from university laboratories.
No giant pharmaceutical company is ready to invest in
orphan drugs as it will not yield hundreds of millions
of dollars in annual sales and profits - a yardstick for
investments in any drug venture," said Bradley, and
looked quizzically at Tom with one raised eyebrow.

"I have no doubts in the bullishness of pharmaceutical and biotech stocks and investments in the present
day world economy" thought Tom.

"But thereby hangs the catch, our game plan. First
of all, we will have a full seven years patent grace - the
exclusive marketing rights," continued Bradley. "Secondly, the British and the American Food and Drugs
Administration will waive the £150,000 registration
fee as part of their programme to support the development of the drugs for orphan diseases," said Bradley.

Tom listened quietly, processing each detail and its caveats carefully, a puzzle evident on his face. A puzzle more from an inner thought than doubt in what Bradley was explaining. Before now, Tom had often pondered the burden he will go through to bring his plans of clinging to abundance to fruition, but it doesn't frighten him, he knows the blessings and price of freedom, the pride and purpose of working for a cause greater than oneself. The secret of life and happiness as Tom knows it lies in giving oneself small personal challenges and clinging to small personal ambitions.

He knows he will be investing a great chunk of his millions in this project and stands the chance of breaking through and having a hold on real freedom, which he's come to realise comes with wealth. But he knows that being in love with abundance means never to be satisfied with increase.

Chapter 2
South East London
20 July 1999

The usual summer morning norm prevailed in the household when Tom woke up. Rays of the rising summer morning sun were filtering into the room from the permanently half-drawn blinders. The day was still young and the morning aging slowly. Many vehicles hadn't started rumbling the streets of west London. Tom was jerked awake from sleep by the ringing of the alarm clock beside his bed. He opened his eyes, or so he thought and had wanted to muffle the shouting clock by putting it under his pillow, but instead he was paralyzed, unable to raise an arm or make a sound, he felt the presence of a threatening evil spirit beside him in the bed. He tried with all his strength to move or shout as terror vibrated through him but to no avail. He felt a weight pressing and pinning him down, reducing him to a helpless and powerless inferior. He was sure he was not dreaming. He could hear the noises in his household – the cat as it mewed, walking in its feline strides past the chained dog in the kennel, insinuating to the dog that if deprivation of freedom – being chained all night and half of the day is what it takes to be man's best friend, that he, "Eddy" the cat, is satisfied as man's good friend or just a friend if "good" will entail a sacrifice.

Tom mustered the last of his energy, wriggling and pushing at the same time, he broke free, hitting his hand against the edge of the bed, and sending the bedside lamp to the floor. Sweat streamed down his face and chest; an aura of fear lurked around the room as he cuddled at the foot of the bed gasping nervously and puzzling over the episode.

"Nothing is better than first hand experience," he thought.

"From now on, I would never blame any person who would want to read an ominous meaning into this puzzle that is threatening to brand sleep an endangered repose," he thought.

Years back, this sleep phenomenon had been a great contributor to why he and his first wife sold their house and moved. His wife was of the opinion that the house was haunted by evil spirits. Then, she used to experience the phenomenon every other night, and Tom had believed that his wife was fantasy-prone. People talk about it as attacks by witches or an abduction by space aliens, who will subject one to a scientific experiment and then set one free again, just as biologists give anaesthetic shots at animals in the wild to weaken them and collect blood samples, hair, sperm, and tag them with microchips for scientific studies and release them thereafter. But ordinarily tom had read and believed it to be a sleep paralysis disorder explained as the disconnection between the brain and the body as a person is on the fringe of waking, such that when the brain gives orders to the body to move, the body doesn't obey because of the temporary disconnection between the brain, the synapses, the neurons and the body. But after today's experience, Tom believes that it may be true as written in science books and also may be true of some other thing as said by other people. Something, that tries to express and manifest in its own style. He glanced around the room forlornly and went down on both knees and silently offered a prayer of gratitude and thanked God for having saved him from the phenomenon and as usual he thanked God for having made him a He. "They all taught me how not to be a husband. Amen," he prayed and rose.

While brushing his teeth from the overnight sour, he figured out how to spend the rest of the day after the meeting with Mr. Bradley. He will have a round of golf in the club and then see how the stock market closed for the evening. He'd bought a "Put Warrant" with a holding period of six months with the newly listed Strol restaurant warrant in the London stock exchange market. As a Put owner, he betted on the depreciation of the Strol restaurant stocks prices from £100 to worthless within the next six months.

Strol is a subsidiary of Soystrol Company, with a chain of restaurants in England and across other European cities. Tom walked into the kitchen to treat himself to a breakfast comprised of cups of black tea and onion rings, no bacon, no omelette, an indulgence he enlisted since he heard from British and American researchers that flavinoids, a powerful antioxidant contained in onion and black tea could be beneficial to preventing cancer and heart attacks. He mistakenly added milk and sighed, he had always felt that milk would dilute the effect of the ingredients in the cup, though he'd heard that milk doesn't prevent the absorption of flavinoids he didn't want to play with his heart because he believed that only heart attack, cancer or an unfortunate accident could impede his march to his business interest and his determination to peg away at it until success is achieved.

When he arrived at the first floor tea lounge of the Hilton Hotels some hours later, Bradley was already waiting. Tom glanced at the wristwatch strapped to his left wrist. He was quite on time, half a minute ahead of schedule. He offered Bradley his hand and he took it in a firm handshake. He drew a chair and sat down.

* * *

When Tom checked the stock prices movements later in the day after meeting Mr. Bradley, he found out that the share price of medical stent from the Layne and Heller Ltd., where he'd maintained £2m worth of stock for the past months and an additional £1m in the last few weeks, had depreciated. Stents are a medical expandable tube used to repair a damaged aorta. The Strol restaurant share price was appreciating against his bet as a Put owner of the Strol warrant. The Strol Put Warrant investment didn't worry him because he knew what to do with it even before he betted.

Everybody knows that discotheque and nightclub stocks are bullish from mid year to early January, a niche that writers of the warrant banked on when pondering the weirdness of this investor. Tom bet on a nosedive of the three digits, £100 per share Strol stock to below £10 and worthless by early January. Even if he was right in his strategy the writers knew beyond all shadows of doubt that he failed in his timing; they were quite sure he betted wrongly and stands to lose his bet.

* * *

Maybe it's coincidence, maybe it's destiny, or both, but one thing is certain, the 20th of July has never been a good date for Tom, a date that reminds him of the ugly facts of his past. Every day of this date of every year, he's often been whipsawed by disappointments and put-downs of some sort. It is a date of excruciating ensemble of morbid, lonely and incarcerated experience. The mere mention or the thought of this date makes him uneasy as though summoning the date's memory alone might set sirens wailing, handcuffs clinking, baggage packing, doors slamming and coffin hearses rolling. But whatever it is that spites his disgust about this date also fires his ambition for the future.

CHAPTER 3
London, 1993

Before the twentieth day of July 1994, Tom had believed that he had good luck and that the prison yard was not for people as smart as himself. Months earlier to this date, he'd eavesdropped on his manager's telephone conversation. Then he was working with the soy infant formula company — "The Soystrol Ltd". He accumulated a total of 80 hours of tape recording over ten months of eavesdropping, and summoned the Soystrol manager, threatening to ruin his reputation and career and probably put him in jail if he doesn't pay him £500,000 in ransom. Mr. Adams, the Soystrol manager, bluffed him.

"Go to hell, you ain't getting nowhere with that. I'll put him in jail instead," Adams told him and went out of the hotel room where Tom had invited him.

Tom went public with his information but the courts found his evidence to be porous. Tom alleged that Mr. Adams was leaking information about the company's decisions that would affect market prices of the Soystrol stocks to market analysts weeks before making the same facts known to the public. An act he acknowledged as insider trading, but the courts failed to qualify the phone conversations of Mr. Adams as insider trading. Tom was sacked from the Soystrol Company where he had worked as a secretary to the manager for five years, and very narrowly he escaped criminal prosecution for illegal eavesdropping and blackmail. And his subsequent effort to take the irregularities to the Securities Commission was thwarted by Soystrol. He'd wanted the Securities Commission to at least suspend the company from trading stocks, and Mr. Adams removed as the manager.

Tom knew that his dismissal from Soystrol could not be rescinded nor could he win a wrongful dismissal lawsuit against Soystrol. He then decided that, the fight he lost in the law court he would win on an independent front. His plan is plain and set – a plot he has spent lots of time into the nights working out and solving puzzles on how best to launch it. While in his gym getting in shape for the day's business, he cross-checked his plot by mind running it from start to finish, yanking and juxtaposing it against an assumed investigator's sieve. Certain that he was prepared and the plot foolproof enough for him to be entirely comfortable with executing it without retreat, happy it was not fiction nor would it be deferred, he walked up to the mirror. The millionaire in the mirror smiled to him and he ran his hand through his hair and made for the restroom. He collected the necessary doings for cutting and soldering from the dark dank cellar of his house, assembled them on the dining table and headed into the street. The East London Sansbury Department Store was the last he visited. He collected two cans of Soystrol infant formula from the shelf and paid with his credit card at the cashier. Back home, he soaked the four cans of the Soystrol infant formula in cold water for thirty minutes and carefully removed the paper print wrapping round the can without tearing it. He cleanly and carefully cut a 4 x 4 cm square hole on the sides of the cans, thus keeping the seals intact. He dusted the contents with rat poison and soldered the piece back to place. He applied glue onto the sides of the cans and wrapped the already dry paper prints tightly around them. It was late when he finished and slept off. He woke up early, showered and dressed to condone the day's weather. At the Brixton branch of the Sansbury Department Store, as he walked down the aisle to the back across the butchery, his gaze rested momentarily on the banner announcing the sale of cloned beef.

"It has such a melt-on-the-tongue texture," read the ad.

But he couldn't understand how that could be when it's said that cells of a clone are as old as the parent animal. He'd rather older cells give tougher flesh.

"Well, that's a hell lot of molecular biology, not my bag," he thought as he glanced cautiously around to see if he didn't draw second glances before launching his own promo, the one he could give total account of. As he walked across the screen room of the store, he sneaked a peek. The screen watch was busy and alert. He hovered around watching the position of the cameras and then turned into the aisle where the Soystrol infant formula is displayed on the shelf. Backing the camera, he lifted his overcoat slightly and brought out the doctored Soystrol formula from under his armpit and slipped it onto the shelf among the other safe cans. He picked one of the safe normal cans and examined the label as if he is contemplating buying it, while his eyes darted up and down and sideways. Satisfied that nobody saw him, he replaced the can onto the shelf and made his way for the exit. At the East London branch of the Sansbury, the scene was not much different. The screen watch was alert but the flux of shoppers was thick. He slipped the doctored can of Soystrol formula onto the shelf and picked two biscuits from the pyramid display with bio-degradable plastic coverings from the neighbouring shelf, and walked to the cashier, paid and left.

The flux of shoppers at the Kensington branch of the Sansbury Supermarket was at its peak when Tom got there. As he walked across the screen room, he saw the security watch standing by the door faking lucidity with a cup of coffee in his hand. Tom looked into his eyes as he walked past but the eyes, though open, were blurred. He was glad that the unit of Sansbury has not employed the popular daily twenty minutes afternoon nap for its employees. He went down the aisle searching for the

Soystrol formula shelf. He did his thing and left.

Back in his home, he put the fourth can in a small red gift box and enveloped it in a soft wrinkled paper nestled in a small wicker basket encased in a black plastic tied with a red lace. He wrapped the lot in a white gift paper with a ribboned bow. He then put the cute ensemble into a large box and addressed it to the executive board of the Soystrol Infant Formula Ltd. He went to the computer to put the PC stamp on it but hesitated as he fired the computer.

"It could be suicidal," he thought. The bar codes with his digital signature will be a hell of a clue to the investigators just as if he sent it through a dispatcher. Rampant gift bombs have made dispatchers very hawk-eyed in recent times. He'd rather brave the post office lines to buy the traditional stamp and send it by normal post.

He logged onto the Internet instead and through a distant broker he opened two accounts of £2000 each in St. Nevis and Antigua. He wrote a post-dated cheque of £4M from the St. Nevis account to the Antigua account, and made a hard copy notation of the transaction and stored. He got to his feet shoulder high and happy that he'd made a provision for the dividend, the panic he will evoke in Mr. Adams and the Soystrol board members. He imagined Mr. Adams sweating, eyes popped out and nostrils fraying as the experimental rat struggled, twitched and died. As Mr. Adams stormed out of the Soystrol board room and headed for his office to call the cops. As Mr. Adams lifted the earpiece and then dropped it realizing it is not a 911 case, otherwise people will die and share prices of the Soystrol stock will depreciate, and resignation letters submitted.

Tom thought of the change the money to be extorted would bring to his life – a £M change.

"Nothing is as good as new and big money," he said softly.

In front of the mirror, he considered a plastic surgery to sharpen his nose and look more handsome.

"No, I wouldn't need it any longer, it is for the poorer set. As a millionaire I need no industrial nose. I'm not going into show business nor am I running an electoral campaign, no public appeal is needed in my new horizon. Besides, my problem has never been that of handsomeness, it's been that of low budget status," he mused, and went into the bedroom to tart himself up before leaving for the post office.

He came out of the post office all smiles – happy that the first phase of the venture was done uneventfully. Across the street he bought the Evening Times from a newspaper stand and drove home. At home, with both feet propped up on the sitting room table, and both hands thrown behind his head, Tom waded through the details of the just concluded part of the venture. Satis-fied that everything was in order and the next step could be pursued without retreat, he opened the pages of the Evening Times and read.

***

The London Appellate Court has ruled the lawsuit against Soystrol Company Ltd. in favour of the plain-tiff, Mr. Shawl, who is currently serving a Six-year jail term in a London prison, in the case Shawl vs. Soystrol. The Justices reached that the trial judge erred in not considering favourably the argument of Mr. Shawl's lawyers. Mr. Shawl was sentenced to six years in jail for statutory rape of a 12-year old girl. The lawyers had argued that the hormone phytoestrogen contained in the Soystrol infant formula which Stella, Mr. Shawl's victim, consumed in her early infant years was responsible for the girl's early puberty and thus Mr. Shawl's lust for her.

"Had she not matured so early, Mr. Shawl couldn't have been attracted to her," argued the lawyers. The lawyers were using the argument of a group of Cambridge researchers that campaigns to ban soy infant formula, arguing that scientific research had demonstrated that the phytoestrogen found in soy milk formula is not good for infants because high phytoestrogen levels as are found in soy milk could delay puberty and even cause infertility in boys, and accelerate puberty in girls.

The Soystrol Company have bled millions of pounds in sponsored contra ad campaigns and on rival researchers – the Oxford researchers who acknowledged that what one eats in early life is vital to later development. The Oxford researchers focused on the sure benefits of phytoestrogen but never proved the Cambridge researchers wrong. The lawyers reminded the court that early puberty in girls is a growingly disturbing norm in Britain that must be resolved.

In condemning Mr. Shawl the lower court wrote that Mr. Shawl should have asked Stella's age. But the high court judges ruled that physical maturity and appearance could provoke or impede questions and answers as the case may be, and in Mr. Shawl's case, the girl's physical maturity had confused him as to the age of the girl. Mr. Shawl was awarded his £2m claim. Shawl will be ready for parole in the next months, having served two-thirds of his six years jail term.

"Hallelujah!" said Tom, as he looked up from the paper to stretch his neck. He was well intimated of the case, he was still an employee of the Soystrol Company when the lawsuit was filed.

Mr. Shawl, an Indian immigrant shop owner in East London was speaking over the phone with a friend when Stella walked into his mini convenience store one evening. She walked from shelf to shelf picking her items of choice, occasionally glancing at the piece of paper in her hand – a preference scale drawn by her mother.

"The doctor has recommended massage and a twenty minute repose in a supine position every day for my thigh and back pain. I didn't know that massage could be an expensive indulgence. The first masseur I consulted charged £60 per treatment that would last 30 minutes. I'm looking for a cheaper deal elsewhere," Shawl said into the mouthpiece and listened as Stella approached the cashier's counter. "I will call you back later, let me attend to a client," said Shawl and hung.

He picked each item and passed it on the automatic cash machine.

"£35," he said.

"Everything is expensive nowadays, rarely do we have a discount," said Stella smilingly and reaching her pocket to pay the bill.

"And they said inflation is under control," she added.

"Sorry for intruding, it wasn't an intentional eavesdropping, but I heard you talk about a masseur. I'm a masseur and I charge £20 per session of massage," said Stella. She reached her jeans trouser pocket to pull out a business card – her mother's, and gave it to Mr. Shawl. While he read, Stella fumbled in her pocket as if she were searching for something, she wasn't.

"The telephone number has been changed. This is the old card. I'm sorry, I'll get you the new one tomorrow," she said finally, and collected the card from Mr. Shawl. She wouldn't want her mother to attend to Mr. Shawl when he calls.

"We can start tomorrow if you are ready," she said, pocketing the card.

"Oh, tomorrow is good," replied Shawl happily.

"That's good, tomorrow," said Stella and collected her shopping and made for the exit.

Shawl watched her as she walked to the exit. Stella is about 1.68 metres tall, full breasted, with a mature voice, a shapely hip and a pretty face; she is a woman visually.

"Must be a good masseur," thought Shawl.

The next day Stella took some massage oil from her mother's kit and went to Shawl's shop. Shawl smiled broadly as she walked into the shop. He led her to the far end of the shop. Behind the confectionary shelves is his bedroom; a dressed six springs bed. A standing fan that seemed have never been put to use for years occupied the edge of the cubicle, a fourteen inch Sony TV and clothes hung on a wooden peg on the wall completed the room's ensemble.

"Could you remove your clothes, please," Stella said.

Shawl dutifully did as directed, but removed only his shirt.

"And your pants, too," said Stella.

Shawl obliged and lay down on the bed on his stomach.

Stella went to work; sprinkled massage oil on his bare back, pressed and rubbed, running her thumbs along the small of his back up and down, putting to work all she learned from her mother's massage parlour. She worked down to his thigh and then up until she got to his crotch, touching his scrotum. She paused and waited for a reaction but no verbal or physical reaction arose, just a shower of goose pimples that covered him. She continued down the thigh then up to his back until her fingers ached, a good job she did.

"Could you lie supine, please," she said to Shawl. Shawl obeyed.

She started with his thighs then up to his chest, rubbing his nipples until they became hard. Shawl closed his eyes, his heart beating fast. Stella rubbed downwards until she eased her hand under his underpants and took his uncoiled stiff rod in her palm. Slowly she pulled his underpants down. She rubbed up and down the shaft of his rod, and bent down to suck on it. Shawl moaned out loud in pleasure. Stella then pushed down her underpants to her knees from under her short skirt, and raised her legs in turn as the thong dropped to her ankles. She flung it aside and climbed onto Shawl on the bed, guiding him into her and rocked him to orgasm. When it was over, Shawl had never felt more relieved.

"Comprehensive massage," he murmured.

Out in the shop he gave Stella £20.

"Let's have another session tomorrow, same time," he said.

"Try and buy the massage oil, and you will have a £2 discount," Stella replied.

"OK," said Shawl.

Out in the open, Stella walked up the street and turned right into another street and to the end of it before crossing into the adjacent street to a Council building. She walked up the stairs to the first floor and pressed the bell to flat number 10. The door opened instantly and she eased into the flat. The lady by the door shut it and hugged her warmly.

"Where have ya been?" she asked enthusiastically. "It's been almost four months ya disappeared. Are ya alright?" she asked.

"Yes I am, and you?" replied Stella.

"So-so," said the lady. "Crack or powder?" she asked.

"How is the powder?" asked Stella.

"The usual stuff," said the lady.

"Give me the crack," said Stella, handing her a £5 note and took her seat next to the window. The lady disappeared into the next room. She was back in two minutes and handed Stella her dose.

Stella was in a tense drugged mood when she got home that evening. Her mother noticed it but kept her cool. She wept bitterly. She'd thought that Stella had quit using drugs. The next day when Stella left the house at 3:00 p.m., her mother waited some minutes before trailing her. Jane waited on the other side of the street out of direct view as Stella entered Mr. Shawl's shop. She came out of the shop after one hour and half. They did make another appointment for the next day. Stella made her way up the street to the drug joint to obtain her dose. Jane followed her daughter patiently back home but didn't ask her a thing. She had found out all she needed – where the money came from. Last four months when she stopped, it was because her teenage boyfriend was thrown into jail for car stereo theft and now she resumed again because she had scratched up another source of cash.

"You cut the roots, not the branches, when you want to kill a tree," Jane thought.

The next day Jane waited for thirty minutes from across the street before she tiptoed into Mr. Shawl's shop. She heard a deep soft moaning of pleasure obviously from an adult, wafting across the shop from behind the confectionary shelves. She tiptoed out of the shop and dialled 911. The police arrived at the scene in five minutes. Shaw was caught red handed having sex with a 12-year old girl and was arraigned before the court for statutory rape. He contested it when told that Stella was only 12 years old. Shawl was sentenced to six years in prison.

When Mr. Shawl filed his lawsuit against Soystrol, Tom and colleagues believed that Shawl was a shameless pedophile.

"Marvellous!" Tom said to himself looking up from the page of the Evening Times. It means there will be an emergency executive board meeting tomorrow morning. And the parcel he's just mailed will be delivered at the company around 10 am, at about the time the board meeting starts.

"What a prime timing," he thought gleefully. That would be a very good hour to launch his ransom call. It would give more weight to the threat and panic his call would evoke.

"They will pay quickly," he thought.

CHAPTER 4
Paris, France
June 1994

Tom checked the daily weather-watch, it wasn't going to be a bright day but nonetheless he got ready for the day's business. He put a call through to the neighbourhood taxi ranch and waited by his front door while rehearsing his ransom speech by mind,

"It is £5M no bargain. The money must be deposited today before 4:00 p.m. and I will call back to let you know where to collect the rest of the cans from store shelves in and around the U.K. You can test the can in your possession on a lab animal to have an idea of what you are up against. Call the shots? The choice is yours," he rehearsed.

The taxi hooted and pulled up in front of his house.

Tom took his seat in the back passenger seat.

"Waterloo station," he said, as he fastened his seat-belt.

At Waterloo station, he paid the driver and got into the station and bought a Eurostar train ticket at the ticketing counter to Paris. He spent the next twenty minutes before departure walking from stall to stall, fingering clothes and ties he had no intention of buying. It took the train two hours speeding through the channel tunnel to Paris nord. Tom hired a mobile phone under a false name on alighting from the train. No identity is required to hire phones, just enough deposit to cover the cost of the phone.

Tom checked the time. It was 9:45 a.m. The parcel must've been in the Soystrol Company premises or would be there in the next fifteen minutes at most. And, judging from his experience in the company, it would be another hour and fifteen minutes before the executive board meeting start. He waved a taxi to the Alma bridge where he mixed with other tourists in their slingy gowns and elegant jumpsuits as they roamed the bridge, chatted on cell phones and leaned on the side rail of the bridge to take pictures and gazed at the giant male stature on the Seine River, the statue the French use to traditionally measure the river's height.

Tom glanced at the cell phone in his hand as its red light blipped, and pressed the off button to save the battery.

"At least from here, Paris, the home investigator will have a hard run for any clue to the calls."

For the one hour thirty minutes he spent perambulating the Alma bridge waiting for the executive board of the Soystrol Company to assemble, the Seine River rose about two inches that could be seen from water level on the giant male statue. The water was just a few centimetres short of its waist. Tom had never heard of the Seine River in a faster tide.

He put on the tooth-like voice-altering clip to his incisors, switched on the cell phone, breathed deeply in and pressed the UK code numbers and then the Soystrol Company numbers. The call was answered at the first ring. A lady's voice came over the line welcoming his call.

Tom recognized the voice to be that of Gladys, the company's receptionist.

"Mr. Adams, please," Tom said.

"Mr Adams is in a board meeting," she replied.

"It is urgent, please put me through to Mr. Adams and the rest of the board members," insisted Tom. "And tell Mr. Adams to put the phone speaker on so that the whole board will hear what I have to say," Tom added.

"Who am I speaking with, please?" requested the lady.

"Not even Mr. Adams or the rest of the board members would want to know who I am. It is urgent, remember, now put me through to them," Tom demanded.

Gladys obliged.

"Who is it?" demanded Mr. Adams.

A thrill of joy ran through Tom that Adams didn't know it was him, Tom. That Adams didn't know the hell he, Tom, was about to unleash on him and the Soystrol establishment. The onslaught had just begun – his onslaught, his revenge.

"Is the phone speaker on? If not, switch it on now."

"But who am I . . ." said Mr. Adams.

"Do as you are told, I haven't got so much time," said Tom.

"But. . ." Mr. Adams protested, hesitated and then obliged, switching the phone speaker on.

Tom was quite on time because the executive board members were contemplating inviting the bomb disposal unit of the Scotland Yard to open the parcel, considering the new wave of parcel and letter bombs in the city of London in the recent times.

Mr. Charles Strong, the Soystrol chairman, waved the messenger who brought the parcel away as Tom's voice rattled out from the speaker. Tom cleared his voice out loud from his corner at the Alma bridge, and made his threat, said his ransom quite clearly and audibly.

"I will call back at 4:05 p.m.," he concluded and hung.

Panic reigned in the board room.

The board members knew the scores of the threat. Britain was in an epidemic of food poisoning and ten children had died within a month of consuming milk from a rival infant formula company, laced with insecticide. Class action lawsuits were rearing their heads at the rival company. Managers and directors were resigning to take the blame for the tragedy. And Soystrol was already suffering from discrimination triggered by the Cambridge researchers' assertion and Mr. Shawl's legal victory over the company. And the British society was

on its threshold of tolerance with infuriating behav-
ioural problems arising from precocious puberty in an
age when mothers, in the bid to reduce breast's down-
ward bound from gravity and breast feeding, use infant
formula more than ever to feed their babies. And now
it's a food poisoning threat to Soystrol. They all knew
that they better find a silent solution to this threat.

Tom left the Alma Bridge, went to the Paris nord area
and found an Internet café and logged onto the bank's
site and to his account in the far away Caribbean islands
to check the movement in his account, but nothing yet.
He waited.

At 3:45 p.m., memos and decisions have been taken,
edited, rejected, re-edited and concluded. All leakable
channels of the incident to the press and public and the
looming danger have been successfully blocked and
despite the fact that the said £5M ransom money have
been electronically transferred to the said account in
the Caribbean island, and as such a deal imminent as
the extortioner promised, tensions still remain high
among the Soystrol executives.

It was 3:58 p.m. when Tom revisited the bank's site
and then his account. His heartbeat quickened as ideas

fleeted through his mind on seeing the figures in his account.

At 4:01pm, he called the Soystrol executive board and told them where to find the poisoned cans of Soystrol infant formula. He dislodged the battery from the phone and threw it into the street bin. He wouldn't want to risk showing his face a second time to the guys at the phone hire office. He'd rather lose his deposit.

Tom went back to London, gloating over his success. He wasn't sure what made him gleeful – the success of the deal? The money? The revenge? All of them.

The deal is done and there is no banging on his door, no plain cloth detectives marauding the street of his neighbourhood, and he is a millionaire.

Bringing the money back to the U.K. is good because Britain doesn't tax any money brought into its economy but only the ones generated locally, but it will raise eyebrows, so he decided against bringing it back to the U.K.

CHAPTER 5
London
July 1994

Absence of income tax, plenty of sun, warm water, surfing and golfing have always been Tom's idea of a paradise. He will relocate to the Caribbean Islands, find himself a seaside big house with lush gardens, plants and trees. He'll wake up every morning to the songs of tropical birds, exercise while a house-help sets his breakfast in the garden in his seaside mansion.

He will build his company and live his life in the Islands. He can register a company within 24 hours and needn't file annual return and accounts. He'd buy a Class A banking license and start private banking, tax and financial planning. He will help to manage the more than $80 billion in so-called illicit money in the

Caribbean. And with luck will steal enough from it. If for any reason the Islands become dangerous for him to continue, he'll move back again to England and buy himself a stately home in the best neighbourhood west of London, buy a yacht and a private jet, get married and have lots of children – eleven of them, just two daughters. By this time, no eyebrows will be raised.

A grand life has been Tom's dream and ambition. When he was a first grader, his teacher, a soft-spoken lady from Wales once asked the class what each of them wanted to be when they grew up.

"A journalist," said little Francis in the first row seat of the class.

"A pilot," said Brent.

"An engineer," said Max.

"A chemist," said Boyle.

"A millionaire," said Tom at his turn.

"Yes, Tom, it's good to be a millionaire, to have a lot of money, but what will you like to study or take up as a profession?" said the teacher.

"I want to be wherever money is. To be a millionaire is all I want," Tom replied stubbornly.

"Tom, there is no doubt to the goodness of money

and what it could buy and where it flows, but you have to have a means of earning it. Being a millionaire is an ambition I'm sure most people nurse, but first of all you need a profession – a musician, film star, TV star, sportsman, doctor, money manager, a whatever – anything to create a channel for the money to flow, otherwise you find it difficult getting there and worse still you corrupt the ambition," said the teacher.

"So?" added the teacher.

Tom looked across the faces and eyes that were fixated on him.

"A millionaire, making money," Tom replied numbly to the derision of the class.

While Tom was planning and executing his future by mind, the Soystrol investigators lit their candles and went to work. They collected the poisoned products from the Sansbury Department Store shelves. From the serial numbers on the cans, they found out the products were among those produced and distributed months ago, sold to the Sansbury stores from whose shelves they were retracted. Sansbury management affirmed that the product had been sold and only reintroduced into the store shelves. Using the digits and computer code prints on the products they adduced that the products were sold the same day at different times and paid for with the same credit card - a credit card that belonged to one Mr. Tom Tobby. When the Soystrol folks heard that Tom Tobby's card was used to pay for the products, they had no doubt that Tom pulled the job. But the detectives knew better; Credit cards could be cloned and used without the owner being aware. Few judges will convict an accused on a credit card links alone. So the investigators kept a 24-hour vigil on Tom and his activities. They culled and regurgitated his electronic mails. He'd just bought a plane ticket to Antigua Caribbean Islands on a British Airways flight. He'd be travelling single on a Wednesday.

On the Wednesday, Tom was sitting in the Terminal 2 departure lounge of the Heathrow Airport waiting for the boarding announcement, his bag propped on the seat next to him and his briefcase rested on his thigh. The briefcase contains all the documents and diskettes, all the information he needed to start a new life in the Caribbean with his newfound wealth. Every passing minute of his waiting gleefully enriches his perception of what he'd done to excel. He knew how much he would miss England, but his is luxury immigration. He now realized that really there are very few honest reasons for being offshore. Most people offshore are either avoiding tax or the highly irritating poke nosing of the British intelligence about how and how not one made his fortune. He saw a man coming towards him. He paused and readied but the man paused briefly in front of him and walked on. Minutes later, a tall white lady with an Arabic nose that looked in her early thirties approached him.

"Could you please accompany me to the office sir?" said the lady to Tom while brandishing an identity card, her voice strictly formal and English.

Tom looked up at her, he saw it in her eyes she wasn't suggesting it to him as it sounded, she was telling him, ordering him to follow her to her office, her eyes steady on his face as he studied her.

"What for?" asked Tom.

"For questioning, sir, the police," she said, and glanced at the identity card she was holding up to plain view in her hand. Tom followed her gaze to the police identity document and he knew immediately that it had something to do with Soystrol, the extortion, the Caribbean accounts and his immigration. There was no other crime he'd committed in recent times to invite such an adversarial approach from the airport police. He was quite sure he'd closed all the tracks to his guilt, but guilt was creeping into him and struggling for control with his calculated outward solid calm, as he got to his feet to accompany the lady to the airport police post.

Tom was frisked and his luggage searched. His passport, ticket, the diskettes, notes and write-ups and his diary were seized.

He was told of his arrest.

"You are under arrest. You have the right to remain silent. Anything you say now will be used against you. You have the right to a lawyer," said the police officer.

Tom called his lawyer using the police phone. Tom was arraigned before a magistrate court judge within 24 hours, charged with extortion. He was shaken but sure he was very elaborate in planning and executing the plot and even more so in cleaning the tracks. He told his lawyer to base his defence argument on the facts that his credit card was cloned, that on the said date of the purchase of the products that he, Tom, was in Brussels. That day, Tom had gone to Heathrow Airport after buying the first can of Soystrol infant formula from the Brixton branch of Sansbury. He had bought a one-way ticket to Brussels a day earlier from a travel agency in his neighbourhood. At the Heathrow airport, he checked in at the Sabena airways check-in counter, obtained his boarding pass and joined the boarding queue. He was seated on an aisle seat beside the door in the 1980 Sabena Airways Boeing aircraft. He stayed seated until the last routine precautionary announcement before take-off.

Fasten seat belts lights were alight and passengers were adjusting their seats to the upright positions. The captain was welcoming passengers on board, his voice wafting from the overhead speakers, an air hostess stood by the aircraft's doorway wearing a fixed professional smile. Tom got up from his seat just as the aircraft's door slowly began its closing arc. He left the aircraft in two steps as the flight attendant stretched to guide the door along its 180° swing to the bolts.

"Sir?" she inquired.

"I'm not travelling, I forgot something very important," replied Tom, already in the tunnel. The door closed and the flight rolled out onto the runway. Tom didn't collect back his ticket coupon for refund or reuse and his name remained on that day's manifest amongst the travelled.

But James, the lawyer, refused the idea, saying, "A return ticket would've been a more robust alibi."

Tom again told James, his lawyer, to insist on the computer voice test of the said taped conversation of the extortionist with the Soystrol executive board against his voice. Because, he, Tom, didn't make no call to anybody, that the computer's graphic detail will show the difference in the pitch and frequency of the voices, but James refused, arguing that if finally found guilty, he will be additionally charged for conspiracy because the court would believe that one of his co-conspirators, still at large, must have made the call.

Tom also suggested that they argue that the money must have entered his account by a simple digit error by the bankers, a common occurrence, and that he, Tom, was going to the Caribbean Islands to resolve it in person. Once again, James said no, reminding him that there is no honest reason for being offshore.

"Then how are you going to get me off this hook?" Tom had asked James in frustration, 'cause he knew that in the three suggested alibis lay the sophistry to liberate him in the court.

"Just wait and see," replied James. "I'm a professional," he added.

During the trial, James pleaded for leniency for his client, arguing that Tom lost his job doing what he believed was in the interest of the shareholders of the company and had a £200,000 character defamation lawsuit against him by Mr. Adams. Tom was found guilty and sentenced to 7 years in jail. As the judge read the sentence, Mr. Adams looked Tom's direction, their gaze met, and Adams raised his finger in a "fuck-you" sign and stuck out his tongue at him, smiling gleefully. Tom gazed murderously at him, and his gaze slowly turned away. He wasn't thinking of Mr. Adams at the moment. James, his lawyer, was his worry because he knew that the court found him guilty not just because he is guilty but because James, the lawyer, didn't prove his innocence. He did only prove to the court why he committed the crime – revenge. He was so sad because the cunt, James, had taken his £30,000 in attorney's fee and promised to win the case. Tom had never trusted an Irishman.

"It is expensive I know, but it's the money you pay to win the case. I ain't just going to the court to represent you in the trial but to prove your innocence," James had told him.

Tom was dragged from the dock and taken to a waiting prison vehicle and taken to the county jail to begin his seven-year sentence.

Tom looked out the air vent of the prison vehicle and saw Londoners, pedestrians and car owners alike going about their daily business without any apparent let nor hindrance – the free citizens, and he, Tom Tobby, chained and to be secluded from the society for the next seven years, tagged dangerous and marked as a criminal forever. Mr. Adams had won again and his bluff fulfilled – an Irish bluff.

"I put you in jail instead," Mr. Adams had told him and stormed out of the hotel room where Tom had invited him for talks. Tom dissolved into tears. He's now very sure that the venture, the manipulation, the money, not even vengeance had been the flame of the game but rather pride, and his ambition. An English pride, a flaming ambition.

CHAPTER 6
England, 1995

In the prison, days turned to weeks, to months, and years. It is sad how prison eats up one's time, but Tom has passed the most difficult part of his incarceration and the rage of a captured warrior that had seized him since his arrest and eventual conviction had since subsided and he has accepted the changed fact of life with faith and grace. His ungainly prison garment seemed to have found fitting on his now fattened frame – fattened from the idleness of prison life.

The AIDS patient inmates were more discriminated against now than ever, they are not only restricted to their separate pavilions but also are not allowed to play and exercise in the same playground at the same time with the healthy inmates. This had caused ripples among anti-discrimination folks and in the British parliament.

Tom was in the 6:30 p.m. TV session in the hostel lounge when the idea came into him. A swirl of energy swept around him and he sprung to his feet, it was such a bright idea and he had no doubt it would come to fruition. He left the lounge for his cell as the prison bell chimed the end of the day – the lock up time. His cell, a 4 x 4 metre square cell with a six-spring bed, writing table, a sink set unit and a narrow horizontal set air vent high up on the wall. Tom had been working in the prison infirmary all these months he'd been in prison, where he worked as a cleaner. He had yet another three years before he would be due for parole. The next four months would be the prison's routine annual blood test. Tom knew that he looked so fleshy and healthy to scale through as HIV positive so he spent the next few months swallowing a great deal of toothpaste with fluoride every morning to suspend appetite. He ate only a meagre quantity of lunch and exercised a great deal. He lost 25 kg of weight and his prison garb had a more ungainly hang on his frame than ever before. When the awaited health week came, Tom's blood was sampled and sealed in a test tube tagged with his name and his prison execution number. The blood was stored among other samples of inmates in the prison infirmary blood bank. Tom woke up one morning and went to work early as usual. He cleaned and disinfected the infirmary floors while waiting for the right hour to execute his plot. Dr. Steve had not arrived yet and Nurse Anne was brewing coffee in the kitchen. She was sitting at the breakfast table with her back to the door and a cup of coffee in hand when Tom peeped into the kitchen and tiptoed to her office. He collected the key to the blood bank and tiptoed out the office to the blood bank. He slotted the key into the keyhole and unlocked the door. He eased into the room in its coldness. His eyes darted across the compartments searching for the "G" section of the alphabetically arranged sealed tubes in the cold chamber, until his eyes settled in on tube number twenty: Gabriel Kicke.

Gabriel has been in the prison for one year and four months for theft. He had told Tom that he was HIV positive and had HIV related meningitis. Tom had met Gabriel in the playground before the precautionary segregation measure was adopted.

"I'm here for a smash and grab raid," Gabriel had begun.

"But I'm not a thief. Of course I knew that any hit more than just a slight knock on the glass display windows of the diamond shop west of London would trigger off the shop's security alarm directly wired to the district's police station and then the nearest police patrol van would come to the shop. Besides, I knew that the pieces of diamond on display were not original diamonds. Only a fool will believe that the proprietors will openly display an expensive blue Lesotho diamond and other rare gems from the war torn Angola, Liberia and Sierra Leone just behind a four inches thick transparent glass without any security man in plain view.

"Look, I worked to get here, I deserve to live longer, I'm here to be cured. I'm no thief but rather one more desperate African who risked everything to get to the west but this time not just for a job and food but for a better health, in search of drugs to prolong my breath. My problems started years back in the 1950's in a small hick town west of river Juba when Hailslessor was still the king of Ethiopia and the British Empire still dominated the political power, and North American biopirates prowled the bushes and forests of Africa in search of rare species and micro-organisms. In the days when plants, crops, wild animals and micro species were uprooted and taken away without permit, long before biodiversity agreement was reached at the 1992 Earth Summit held in the South American beach city of Rio de Janeiro, that established the sovereignty of nations over their genetic resources and their entitlement to fair and equitable sharing of the benefits.

"I'm Gabriel Kicke Hailea, Kicke is my maternal grandfather's name, a Madagascan who grew rosy periwinkle in the Majunga city of Magadesca. He died of testicular cancer. May his soul rest in piece," Gabriel said.

"In those days the spreading tentacles of bio prowlers reached my town in Ethiopia. Dad was coming home from his farm on a mule back when he saw some westerners running frantically out from the Juba shrine, blood dripping from their bodies and faces. Daddy knew they must have been attacked by the Juba shrine soldiers since they are not natives and weren't accompanied by any guide from the clan. Daddy stopped and aided them and following Dad's advice they solicited help from the native priest – the Juba priest, to collect barley plants, micro-organisms and some frog species found in the five hundred and fifty meters square sacred bush of the Juba God.

"I've often imagined where Mama might have been at that hour. Probably with her neighbourhood friends or doing her daily household chores in the hay thatched roof house that I was born in. The western bio prowlers had invaded the shrine on their own but had hurried off the bush without any samples. They were furiously attacked by the Juba shrine monkeys, wild bees, slit-tongued viper snakes called the soldiers of the Juba God by the locals. The priest refused the westerners any form of assistance, citing that it is an abomination to take away roots and branches from the shrine to a foreign land and especially to take away the offspring of the Juba god, the frog species.

"Dad spoke fairly good English, English he learnt from my mother who had in- turn learnt from her father who worked for some westerners who had come to Madagascar to collect periwinkle samples to produce drugs for testicular cancer, though granpa eventually died of testicular cancer for not being able to buy the drugs produced from the raw material of his produce.

"When the westerners told Daddy of their meeting with the Juba priest and his refusal to assist them, Daddy believed that the premise of the priest's refusal was wrong. Dad had a bold vision of world health and bio development. In principle he wasn't wrong but the biopirates might think he was wrong and a fool, because that was before fairness in biodiversity became an issue. As the son of the soil, the monkey, snakes and other soldiers of the Juba God have no power over Dad and cannot attack him. The Juba God loves her subjects, her clan. Dad collected litres of water from the Juba shrine brook, plucked some fresh leaves from the shrine and boiled the leaves in the water. On cooling, he gave the westerners the water to drink and wash their body with. Believing what the westerners had told him, Dad promised burnt votive offerings of cows, heifers and horses to the Juba God, and led the westerners into the Juba bush and they collected a good measure of barley species and frog species under the gaze of the shrine monkeys and vipers – the soldiers of the shrine, in defiance of the Juba priest's refusal to cooperate.

"A great blustery wind, lightening, thunder, and the

Juba brook roared out loud as the westerners stepped out the Juba bush with the frog species.

"The villagers flayed my daddy with reproaches. Years passed and the biopirates didn't return to make sacrifice and offerings to the great Juba God as they promised. And based on that, my family was ostracized by the clan. My father later incurred the wrath of the Juba God. He died of diarrhea twenty years later. My mother had died years earlier. I managed my life and lived with the daily reproaches of the ostracized. But things became high and dry for me when I nursed my newly married wife, two months into pregnancy to her death. She died of AIDS related meningitis. My village lacked electricity and pipe born water and I had seen patients turned back from the hospitals because they had no drugs with which to treat them, because the hospitals had no medical supplies of their own to attend to the patients.

"Most of the population relies exclusively on the traditional healer – the Juba shrine priest. As an AIDS patient, I could not be treated by the Juba priest 'cause I'm an outcast whose family incurred the wrath of the Juba God. So when I heard from my small transistor radio that the South African parliament made a law granting the right to drug companies to produce generic drugs for AIDS at lower prices, the African price, to help its infected population, I decided to emigrate to South Africa. I travelled to South Africa by sea, canoeing down river Juba into Somalia and joined a boat at the Somalian port of Giamame to Port Elizabeth in South Africa, then to East London port, and finally to Cape Town.

"In Cape Town, my hope of being cured was flipped when I learnt that South Africa, as a member of WTO, agreed to honour foreign patents and acknowledges it would face trade sanctions for dealing in generics produced before the patent expires. But in her suffocation, South Africa had tried to use the loopholes in the TRIPS – a patent agreement to produce cheap generic AIDS drugs by paying a negotiated royalty to the patent holder – compulsory licensing. However, the effort of the government of South Africa was shackled by the western trade negotiator's threat of trade sanctions against South Africa. Not long afterwards, South Africa was placed under 301 watch list – a prelude to trade sanctions thus eroding my chances of obtaining my own dose of Virodene – the cheap South African made anti-AIDS drug.

In Cape Town I worked in a fruit farm while deciding on the new attitude to enlist to better my health. One day, I decided to hide in a canvas topped steel box container of a cargo ship, the type meant to carry heavy machinery, food and fruits. The container was loaded with crates of fruits and apples to be transported to Western Europe. It allowed just enough air to keep the fruits fresh and me alive for the week's journey across the Atlantic. In the cramped corner, where I hid, I urinated and defecated. My food was apples and vegetables that I picked from the crates in the containers. After what I believed to be three weeks, we arrived at the teeming harbour that I later learnt is called Dover in England.

"The container was taken to a warehouse in London where I stayed for another two days before it was opened. I waited patiently as the workers in the warehouse unloaded the crates from the container, fresher air entering my environment at each removal of the crates. A few crates to my corner, the workers stopped, probably for a short break. With the last strength in me, I pushed the crates to create a space and crawled along, wriggling and forcing my body forward to the open. I got off the container and moved forward on my wobbly feet, which appeared to be having problems carrying my rather frail weight. As I made my way to the gate, somebody saw me and shouted at me.

" 'Stop! And identify yourself,' he shouted.

"I tried to run but I was so faint from hunger and cold. They arrested me and took me to the Immigration office where I applied for a refugee status and it was granted to me after one year of waiting.

"I contacted the Oxford University Medical Centre when I heard they were testing a promising experimental treatment that involves an essential enzyme that props and prolongs the action of the protease inhibitors on the AIDS virus. They accepted and I sent them my medical record and blood samples, but weeks later I was told I could not be included in the programme because the study needed sixteen people: four whites, four Indians, four black and four Orientals, and they've got enough black volunteers and the investor who was sponsoring the venture provided just enough resources for only sixteen patients — who have been promised a life-long support if the drug worked. I had no health insurance and my meagre stipend was barely enough to feed, and my local health authority would not pay for my treatment and drugs. The dream went dead again, so that fateful evening I went to the west of London and waited until the shop owners locked their shops and went home. I smashed the glass window of one shop and grabbed ten diamond rings. Alarms were wailing and I was sure the police were on their way to the shop but I idled around the vicinity waiting for them. I could've made away quite on time with my loot but I waited to be caught, to be arraigned before a magistrate and be jailed so that they will be obliged to cure me. I pleaded no contest when the charges were read out for me in the court. I was sentenced to five years and I have stayed a year and four months and have been receiving my adequate dose of the anti-AIDS cocktail. The other day the doctor told me that the HIV virus count in my blood sample has been reduced, and by the grace of God I will be cured before my sentence finishes. Amen," said Gabriel, crossing himself piously.

Tom looked him in the eyes, in deep thought.

"Amen," he said.

Admittedly Gabriel's story is heartful enough to make anyone be filled with compassion, but Tom knew that Gabriel wasn't hoping for crumbs of compassion.

CHAPTER 7

Tom removed the test tube containing Gabriel's blood sample from its rack. His gaze travelled down the rack chambers in search of the "T" section. He found it, "Tom Tobby", and removed it from the rack. He exchanged the name tag on Gabriel's tube with the tag on his tube, and replaced the tubes into the rack, and turned to leave. As he gripped the door handle to open, he heard footsteps along the corridor. The rhythm of the steps was Dr. Steve's. He waited breathlessly until he heard the clinking of keys and a door opened and closed at the far end of the corridor. He left the room and closed the door quietly and moved forward towards Nurse Anne's office to replace the keys and went out of the office quickly. He heard nurse Anne say "Good morning" to Dr. Steve as she hurried to her office. Tom walked to the cleaners' cart that was idling at the corridor corner and wheeled it busily away.

Dr. Steve, Nurse Anne, and the entire infirmary team have a particular curiosity about Tom's health. Tom has been losing weight at a tremendous rate in recent times. Their curiosity was satisfied after the blood samples had undergone laboratory tests. Tom's blood sample tested HIV positive and the virus count per cubic millimetre of blood was high. Tom noticed that his game came true from the pitiful and compassionate glances he drew in the infirmary. One morning, Dr. Steve summoned Tom to his office. In an effort to deliver the news well, reduce the shock and shore up Tom's psychological defence, Dr. Steve started by asking Tom some questions.

"What does life and freedom represent to you?" asked Dr. Steve.

"A man deprived of freedom is not a living man," replied Tom.

"And health?" asked Dr. Steve.

"Without health life is worthless," said Tom.

"And hope?" asked Dr. Steve.

"The living must be hopeful 'cause hope is like

dreams and when dreams die, life becomes worthless," replied Tom.

"That's great, Tom," said Dr. Steve, tapping his pen on the page of an open notebook before him, thinking of how best to hit the point, quite aware that any haste or ignorance on delivering the news might cause a lot of emotional pain and can even compromise the effectiveness of the treatment that will ensue.

"So you mean that it's of utmost importance to be hopeful 'cause on hope does life hang?"

"Yes, doc," said Tom.

"What do you think of terminally ill patients" asked Dr. Steve.

"Hope and faith," replied Tom.

"And AIDS patients particularly?" asked Dr. Steve.

"Hope and faith," replied Tom.

"What if I tell you that you are HIV positive?" asked Dr. Steve.

"Well, until you tell me," replied Tom.

"You are HIV positive," said Dr. Steve.

"You ain't joking, are you?" said Tom.

"No, I'm serious, your blood sample shows you are HIV positive," Dr. Steve said and watched as furrows lined Tom's face into gloom and two face lines stretched nearly to the edges of his nostrils forming a bracket around his mouth, as his face puckered up and he cupped his hands to his face and sobbed, tears streaming down his cheeks.

"What a good actor you are," a mind whispered to Tom and he sobbed even more.

Dr. Steve waited, allowing him time to cry.

"I bet if this piece of acting is put up for an Oscar contest, you will win the best actor award," said a mind to Tom.

When he sobered up Dr. Steve walked round the office desk to him and rested his right hand on his shoulder.

"It is not always as bad as we think," he consoled.

"Take the day off," he told him.

At the doorway Tom paused, crossed himself and looked over his shoulder at Dr. Steve.

"Thank you, doc," he said.

Dr. Steve nodded his welcome, satisfied at Tom's comportment, happy that he delivered the bad news very well, that the patient was not harbouring any negative feelings.

Tom made his way to the hostels, struggling not to show his glee because the game was not yet over. In his cell, he pulled up into the air several times, punching the air in triumph and joy. By the next morning, he was taken to the HIV positive inmates hostel and furnished with cocktail medications that he never swallowed. By the following week, Tom had written and posted a hand written request for a Prime Ministerial pardon based on ill health. He outlined how terminally ill he was and pleaded that having served more than one-sixth of his total sentence that he wished to spend the last days of his life beside his loved ones – friends and family. He expressed remorse for having committed his crime. Weeks later, Tom's request was granted by the Downing Street Clemency Board. Tom went back to the streets of England a free citizen.

CHAPTER 8
London, 1996

Things didn't change as much as Tom had thought. It was still the same old city of London. The more it changed the more it remained the same. The thought of Gabriel always gave Tom goose pimples and triggers his imagination about the huge desperation that spanked him into crossing the Atlantic cramped in a cargo ship container meant for inanimate items to west Europe to be able to obtain his daily dose of anti-HIV drug cocktail.

While navigating for information in the Soystrol share information site, Tom found out that Mr. James' family had maintained a 3% shareholding of Soystrol stocks for the past ten years and had disclosed it only some four months ago, long after his, Tom's, trial and conviction. The London stock exchange made it adequately clear that such percentage of shareholding in any company must be reported to the exchange commission who will in turn make it public.

"No wonder James had submitted the stupid plea he knew would earn me no compassion, he must've reached that my acquittal and probable new offensive on Soystrol Company would bring a bit of fall in the share prices of the Soystrol Company. He didn't mind the psychological violence, the horror I would go through in jail, even after paying him £30,000 in legal fees," Tom thought.

Tom's .45 calibre was one of his old possessions that was still intact after his eleven months' absence from the streets of the free world. The short gun was safely hidden inside the shaft of the bottom newel post of the staircase in his house, a house he bought through mortgage from the public housing project in the 1980's. He'd handed the house over to an estate agent to manage within the time of his aborted relocation bid to the Caribbean Islands to his newfound wealth. It was a new and shiny silver .45 automatic, fitted with a silencer.

Through his estate agent, Tom had informed his tenant who was already two months behind with his rent that he would have a routine inspection of the property as contained in the contract.

Mr. Christmas, the tenant was in his place of work when Tom turned the handle on the front door of the Victorian house. And pushed the door open, stepping into the four meter long corridor that was dominated by the staircase that elevated to the rooms above. He closed the door behind him and walked to the staircase. Holding the round top of the new white painted newel, he looked up the stairs, admiring the new and clean carpet. To his left was the door to the sitting room, above the doorway to the sitting room was a flowerpot from where a creeping flower plant twined along a guiding rope down the remaining length of the corridor towards the kitchen.

"He must be a neat and organized man. And for the flowers, probably he's also sentimental. Good," Tom thought, as he went into action.

Holding the round top of the newel with both hands, Tom twisted to the right and left to break the oil paint coating. He pulled it upwards with much force, lifting it off. He dipped his hand into the hollow and held the rope tied to a nail driven into the wood and pulled up the rope. The weight assured him that his gun is still in place. He held it as it came into view and he loosened the knot of the rope tied around it. He placed the gun on the first step of the staircase and replaced the round top of the newel onto the top of the shaft and pushed it into place. He moved two steps backwards and inspected it. It was in order, no visible cracks.

Holding the .45 calibre in his hand, Tom smiled loonily. The gun was still well oiled and loaded, he pushed back and forth the safety catch and aimed.

"Good," he murmured to himself and buckled the gun onto his waist belt and walked to the restroom and washed his hand and face. He looked himself up in the mirror and smiled in satisfaction. He left the room and made for the front door. He walked out the front door, closing it behind him, and turned the key in the lock.

CHAPTER 9

Tom was given a form to fill in the lobby of the office building where barrister James maintains a private law office. He waited as the lady behind the desk put a call through to James' office to announce his visit. She filed the filled visitor's form and provided Tom with a visitor's badge, which Tom put into his breast pocket instead of clipping onto his jacket to plain view.

The lady waved him forward to the elevators where a security man holding a metal body scanner was screening a visitor before letting him board the elevator car, a routine adopted by most tall office buildings in London since Scotland Yard received intelligence that the IRA might resume bombing campaign on the mainland Britain. Tom walked past them into the elevator car and waited. The security man looked him over, and as he didn't see any visitors badge on him, he didn't say anything, believing he must be a worker in one of the numerous offices in the building. Tom pressed the button to the fourteenth floor and the elevator started its ascent.

At the fourteenth floor, Tom stepped out and walked forward to James' office. There were about four people in the waiting room. He took his seat and waited. The secretary approached him from the inner office with a fixed smile and offered him a tag. Tom was the visitor number ten of the day.

"You are welcome," she said. "You will soon be attended to."

James took a deep drag on the Havana cigar and let out a thick plume of smoke as the secretary ushered Tom into the office. Surprise and fear suffused him as he recognized Tom, his eyes scanning him nervously. He'd thought Tom was somewhere in the dungeon of British prisons, but here was Tom, sure and menacing.

"Tom?" he called out.

"Yes, it's me, Tom."

"What happened?"

"I had a Prime Ministerial pardon."

"Since when?"

"I have been on the streets for a couple of days, but it's just today I decided to visit some of my debtors to collect overdue debts and see if I could reorganize my life and put things in order once again," said Tom.

"Are they paying?" asked James.

"Well, I will know after this session here, I'm starting with you James", said Tom.

"Pardon?" said James, frowning.

"Sometimes, it is irritating how time changes things. I've never known you to be deaf, James. I mean I'm starting my debt collection with you," Tom said.

"Tom, I have many clients to attend to, come back here when you are more sober," said James, and started getting up but paused halfway on seeing Tom brandish a .45 calibre and waved him down.

"Sit down," said Tom sternly.

James slumped into his chair agape.

"I'm dead serious James, I'm not here for jokes."

"I do not owe you, Tom," said James, plaintiveness in his voice. "And please put away the gun," he added.

"I wouldn't have needed it if not for the fact that you

will be much more rational before it. You had just start-ed bluffing. With it you don't bluff, dare you?"

Silence.

"Answer me, cunt!" shouted Tom, rising from his seat. James saw the madness in his eyes.

"No," he said, raising his hand above his head in a gesture of surrender.

"Good, you dare not bluff or fuck with me. Here and now, I want my money, my £30,000," said Tom.

Silence, as they studied themselves, Tom stern, sure and menacing. And James was quiet and retreating.

"James," Tom said finally. "I know I will make more money from you in a civil law suit but I need money ur-gently. Besides, I don't want any of my money to get into the pockets of your likes, scoundrels. I'm not here to rob you but rather to collect the money you conned out of me. I mean the money you extorted from me while pretending to be representing me as my defence lawyer in the extortion charges against me – Tom vs. Soystrol. I'm here to take my money back.

"I will not charge you any interest nor will I charge you for the psychological violence and horror I went through in jail. I will only add the one per cent inflation rate. Believe it, if I had known that your family had a 3% undisclosed share holding of the Soystrol stock, I wouldn't have contracted you as my defence attorney in the criminal case brought against me by the Soystrol Company," said Tom.

"What do you think you are doing? Muscling me? And what do you think you are? Smart? Look – I'm a criminal lawyer, our shareholding with Soystrol have been reported to the London Stock Exchange whose duty it is to make it public through its regulatory news service," said James.

"That's before or after I contracted you to defend me, where instead of defending me you submitted a plea bargain that stinks to high heavens, and I was thrown into jail. Remember, you promised not to bluff," said Tom, waving the gun. "James, I have never held myself out to be a great genius or a paragon, but I'm plenty smart, hope it answered your question," said Tom.

"Well, I'm not here for arguments, I'm here to receive my money and now," added Tom, tapping the nose of the gun on the table. He rose and moved the gun closer to James' face.

"At one percent inflation rate, my cash will be

£30,300. Here", he said, stretching his open left palm into his face.

James opened his drawer and brought out a cheque-book and started writing.

"I need cash, no cheques," said Tom.

"I have no cash here, Tom," pleaded James, the madness in Tom's eyes making him even more nervous than the short gun in his hand. "But my banker is a few floors above," he added, nodding upwards. "The cheque can be cashed within minutes by the messenger."

He finished writing the cheque and stretched to press the white button at the far edge of his table to call the attention of the office messenger.

"Wait a minute!" Tom shouted. He lowered the gun out of sight under the table where he aimed directly at James' groin.

"Any smart move, James, you will be the first to die. I blow you up, make no mistakes," threatened Tom.

The messenger came hurrying into the office room. James handed him the cheque.

"Cash this cheque in the bank upstairs," James ordered as the messenger took the cheque from him.

There was tense calm as they waited. The messenger

came back into the office after some twenty-five minutes with a Barkley's Branch Polyethylene bag full of cash. He placed it gently on the desk and disappeared into the outer office.

Tom crouched forward, reaching the bag. He opened it and brought out the square block of cash sealed in a transparent soft plastic. Tom ripped the seal open and the crisp smell of the mint greeted his nostrils. He brought out a bundle and felt the texture of one of the bills. Satisfied, he put the bundle back into the plastic and into the bag.

"Do you have any extra briefcase here?" Tom demanded.

"Yes I do," replied James and started getting up then paused. "Could I?" he asked.

Tom nodded his yes.

James got up, pushed back his chair and moved halfway across the office to the cupboard beside the transparent glass French window overlooking the street below. Tom moved the gun, aiming at him as he moved. He opened the large cupboard and brought out a black leather combination lock briefcase. He left the cupboard open and walked back to his chair and placed the briefcase on its belly and watched as Tom tucked the money into it.

"What's the number?" Tom asked before closing it.

"Six, three, four, right and zero, zero, four for left," said James.

Tom tried the number out with the briefcase open before locking it. He grabbed the case by its handle, eased out of his seat with the gun still pointing at James' forehead.

"Nobody robbed you, James. I've just taken back my money. You did me no service, you have no right to the money," said Tom, stepping backwards.

"It's not your money, Tom. It's Soystrol's money," replied James.

"Yes, of course, the only drop they didn't collect from me, who knows, to pay you to fuck me up," said Tom.

"Never mind, Tom, I know how to forget about everything and relax. That's nothing you've taken from me. I will still make even more from people like you, idiots, criminals, fools," said James.

Tom paused at the doorway, his eyes fixed on James.

"Tell me, James," he said, stepping back into the office. "Next time if a client of yours has a court case with a company where you and your family have shareholdings and his case and eventual victory will affect the share prices of the company stock, especially to your financial disfavour, will you tell the client about your allegiance with the company so that he hires another lawyer and with luck save himself the psychological torture of the prison yard? Or will you be callous as you were with me, not minding what might become of him in jail?" Tom asked, a mad glint in his eyes.

James kept mute but looked Tom over and blinked.

"Tell me, James!" barked Tom, waving the .45 calibre. "Will you?" he added.

"Yes, I will," answered James.

"You will tell him or you will be callous?" asked Tom.

"I will tell him."

"Good!" said Tom, and turned to go, then paused to sheath his gun. He crossed the doorway into the outer office and was gone.

No client of James or any person in recent memory has ever made him so frightened, vulnerable and defenceless.

CHAPTER 10

In the hotel room where he'd been lodging since his release from prison, Tom counted and recounted the money in delight.

"I served time for the crime I committed but I didn't lose any penny on the attorney," he thought.

Tom knew it was time to replace outdated ideologies with new vision premised on enduring values. He'd contemplated extending his wealth seeking well into capital ownership via West end – the London Stock Exchange using the new democratised world finance. Two weeks crawled by before Tom found himself a flat to live in, and began his rooting as a member of the London stock market gentry. He obtained a two months training from a day trading firm and was offered a desk and computer in the firm. Tom entered the securities business as a day trader, trading on stocks full time, buying and selling small quantities of extremely volatile tech stocks, holding them for hours and at times only minutes before selling them. In three months, he discovered a perfect system of investing and betting on stocks, and increased the volume of stocks he traded as his luck in the business flourished.

Prison is now a distant memory and the scar of it no longer fresh, except for Gabriel with whom he exchanges letters every so often. In the last letter Tom received, Gabriel had written:

"The doctors have declared me cured, it was a miracle. I've been removed from the AIDS patients' hostel and now reside in the hostel for healthy inmates. I use the same playground and at the same time with the healthy inmates and a thanksgiving service was observed in the prison chapel on my behalf last Sunday. It is a miracle. Tom, please read John II verse 35, and glorify the Lord for he is great," wrote Gabriel.

Tom was really touched. He knew that the ripples of his swindle had spread to a dangerous extent. He contemplated writing the prison infirmary to tell them to have another test on Gabriel. He was afraid that Gabriel's health condition would worsen 'cause he would now be omitted from the necessary treatments in the belief he'd been cured. But he decided against it on remembering that nothing cures better than faith.

"Nothing really cures better than faith, remember," a mind had told him. Tom was so surprised and disappointed that the medical personnel were so gullible as to believe that a person who had been terminally infected months ago by an HIV related infection could be totally free from the HIV virus just like that. But more surprised were the prison infirmary workers − doctors and nurses, who had expected a reduction in the viral load in the patient's blood sample at best, and not a total disappearance of the HIV virus from his blood stream. Nonetheless, they continued supplying Gabriel with his dose of cocktail of drugs but never bordered to have another test of his blood sample. They believed that the HIV viruses in Gabriel's blood stream must've mutated into a non-virulent virus and then recognized, attacked and quickly cleared by the body's blood CD_4-T cells. While they waited for the next opportunity to test Gabriel's blood sample, Gabriel was slowly but steadily being cleared of the virulent HIV virus and opportunistic infections by faith. His natural immune response was reinforced more than ever, as his white blood cells engulfed and strangled out the HIV viruses in his blood stream and lymph nodules. Gabriel became free of AIDS virus just by a strange twist of fate occasioned by a selfish manipulation by Tom the extortionist.

CHAPTER 11

Tom came back to his house at 9:30 p.m., having completed the day's schedule, happy that the 20th of July was almost gone, the most boring day of every year for him. As he lay on his bed, he was sure that it wasn't a breach of courtesy that he didn't go to lay flower and sooth séance in the cemetery. Though he'd never hated any of his wives nor had he ever envied men who are successful in marriage and others who can con women to their sides and make them spend their fortunes with them, fortunes from outlived husbands, family inheritance, hard work and sometimes feminine-assisted earned fortunes, but with women, Tom, had always suffered pain. It's always him that bears and feels the pains of the relationships.

The callous bunch he had once called wives had all walked out on him on flimsy excuses and never came back. Excuses as flimsy as the duration of their sexual intercourse – this was the case of his first wife, Alice, his childhood friend who had always wanted him erect if possible for twenty-four hours of every day. Alice had argued throughout their marriage that Tom often surrendered in bed long before her. That he, at least, has to hold it for ten minutes into the act before spitting. With time, Alice's biological and orgasmic clock readjusted diminutively to five minutes into sexual intercourse before orgasm, the minimum time most young women could condescend to, but Tom hardly held it up to three minutes and had refused and discharged the suggestion to see a urologist for premature ejaculation therapy. Alice, a natural woman whose interest in men premised on love, family and sexual satisfaction, opted for separation.

Twice Tom had got married and twice he was divorced but had never paid for his divorce, the ladies had often paid except for his first wife, Alice, who died while they were still married on paper though separated, and as such Alice saved herself the divorce expenses.

Kate was Tom's second wife. She is not a College graduate nor a beauty queen. Kate grew up believing that women who are born less than conventionally attractive are the throwaways of the womenfolk and those with above average charm should control and enslave their men. She'd skilfully mastered the act of conning men into her world and made them empty their coffers on her and her lesbian sweethearts. In those unpleasant days of his marriage, Tom was sitting on the cushion in the living room ruminating on the market losses of recent times, on how to get up financially again, and brooding on the verse he'd read from the Bible when Kate came into the sitting room and, standing before him,

"I want a divorce," she said.

Tom looked up at her, blinked and shook his head.

"Okay, I will give you a divorce, but you pay for it," said Tom, quite unlike other times she had asked for divorce, when Tom had tried to convince her, telling her how much things would change and it would be alright. But now, Tom has understood Kate very well. Kate was a deliberate high flyer who only joined a roaring tide. Since understanding Kate, Tom has not expected any less from her. Kate is not a hard-time wife, not the type that builds any man a backbone.

"Why me?" asked Kate.

"That's the dumbest question I've ever been asked," said Tom.

"You don't need to be rude, just tell me why?" replied Kate.

Tom turned and glared at her. "I don't want to divorce you, you want to divorce me. So you pay for it. Why must I pay for being dumped?" said Tom.

Kate turned and walked into the room. She packed her belongings and left the next morning. When Tom received the divorce notice from the divorce court, Kate's allegations were infuriating. Kate had alleged infidelity, domestic violence and irresponsibility.

But it was him, Tom, not Kate, who came back one Friday afternoon, unlocked the front door and tried to push it open but the door was held shut by an inner latch. Tom pressed the doorbell and waited for almost fifteen minutes before the door was finally opened. Sitting on the couch, wearing a nervous, if impugn expression and scattered hair was Beatrice, Kate's bosom friend.

"Good evening," said Tom and pushed forward to kiss Kate on the lips, but she turned her face and Tom's lips caught her on the cheek.

Tom looked her in the face and noticed a receding suffuse of pleasure, the type of pleasure that often creams her face fifteen minutes into cunnilingus, an act she had often insisted on as a prerequisite to lovemaking – her turn on.

"Good evening," said Beatrice to Tom.

Tom noticed a sexual huskiness in her voice and suspected a sexual impropriety, but refused to believe it, afraid it would upset his rather relatively tranquil family life.

Tom had heard Kate not once moan and groan what often sounded like "beatie" in their lovemaking sessions, especially when she was near orgasm as he licked the edges of her clitoris with his tongue, while clicking her clitoris with his finger, but had always believed it to be one of those sweet nothings that an orgasmised person utters.

"How can she allege unfaithfulness," murmured Tom.

It was him, Tom, who found rumpled sheets of papers in the wastebasket beside their writing table. In the papers, a 'he' was severely disparaged.

"I have never loved him any bit but I only have an unspoken contract with him, an income support contract. I can opt out at will. Remember, I need a financial prop and for now he provides the propping," read one disparaging line in the rumpled letter.

"That's only fiction," Kate had replied dismissively when Tom asked her about the rumpled sheets.

"Fiction?" asked Tom.

"Yes, fiction."

"What sort of fiction, Kate?" Tom had insisted and followed her as she turned and swept out of the room into the sitting room.

"You mean it is fiction?" continued Tom.

"Yes, it's fiction and don't bother me any more with that," retorted Kate.

"I, not you, will be furious," Tom said.

"OK! Go get furious," shouted Kate as she hit Tom twice on his mouth with her fist. Tom swung his hand to hit her back but pushed her away instead. She staggered and fell onto the floor, sprang to her feet and darted into the kitchen and was back into the living room within seconds brandishing a hammer. She hit Tom hard on the head as he turned towards her. He felt an explosion in his head as stars diverged from his eyes, and he slumped to the floor. From then on he remembered not a thing of the lot that followed. When Tom woke up, he was surrounded with roses, his head bandaged and he had a terrible headache. He had no idea how long he'd been knocked out. Kate was beside him, sobbing softly. She bent forward and kissed his forehead as he opened his eyes and she pleaded for forgiveness. Tom forgave her but the issue of the rumpled sheets was never raised again.

"And she alleged domestic violence against me," thought Tom.

Tom had maintained a spousal joint account with Kate, an account that held thousands of pounds, but Kate's spending sprees brought the account to nothing. In her wardrobe, Kate amassed the clothing equivalent of the priciest Jaguar car, jewellery and gold finger and toe nails, earrings and necklaces. The account was in perpetual depletion until Tom stopped shoring it up and it got closed. Then Kate's gold and diamond finger nails, her choicest clothes, earrings and necklaces started disappearing one after the other.

Tom had replaced the house wall paintings and piano several times. Kate had often alleged that she binned them because they had irreparable damages. Tom had suspected a host of things and irregularities but had never seen any evidence of Kate's drug abuse. Kate had skilfully hidden it from him. But one snowy winter night Tom had come home and met Bruce, the Labrador, whining and shaking from cold in the veranda. He'd stroked the dog and opened the door but Bruce refused to enter into the house. He clutched Tom's trousers with his canines and pulled him. Tom stroked him on the head but the dog continued pulling him as he tried to step into the house.

It then crossed Tom's mind that something could be wrong for Bruce's strange behaviour. For starters, the dog was not supposed to be on the veranda in this cold.

"Kate!" he called out, but there was no reply. He became alarmed. He then followed Bruce, who headed for the car and pawed at the driver's door in an effort to open it. Tom opened the door and got into the car and Bruce ran round the car to the passenger's door and jumped in as the door opened. Tom gunned the engine and drove down the street to the main avenue and turned left. As he drove past an intersection down the road Bruce whined and pawed at the glass on the passenger door. Tom turned into the direction and Bruce stayed quiet as they drove down the deserted street until they got to another intersection and Bruce jumped onto the back seat and pawed at the right side glass behind the driver's seat and Tom followed the direction. He followed Bruce's directives as they drove past neighbourhoods until they entered the Brixton neighbourhood. Bruce directed him towards the 'frontline' area of Brixton; the run-down drug-washed neighbourhood of Brixton. Bruce was whining seriously now, his eyes darting here and there across the street until he found her, he whined and pawed the glass, and barked. Tom looked towards his direction and slowed down to a stop. Beside the road, in front of a closed stall, was a figure sitting crouched. Tom opened the door for Bruce and he got down and ran towards the crouched figure, barking and wagging his tail. Tom approached and was showered with goose pimples on recognizing the individual. He touched her. She was cold. He lifted Kate and carried her into the car and drove her to the hospital.

When searched, two wraps of heroin and a stick of heroin- laced cigarette was found on her. She had taken an overdose of heroin. She had pawned her car to obtain her dose as there was no money in the joint account and the credit cards had been blocked. That is the day Tom knew the bitter truth. His wife of two years had been a drug addict all those years without him knowing.

The doctors gave Kate a dose of naxalone to prepare her for naltrexone – used to treat overdose. Kate spent months in the hospital and went through detoxification. Her heroin was stopped and she was put on buprenorphine, a medication that suppresses the agony of withdrawal. She attended lectures during her stay in the hospital and learnt how to shake off the habit and was discharged after six months.

At home, she asked Tom to forgive her irresponsibility and Tom obliged as always.

And in this divorce process, it's him, Tom, who was accused of irresponsibility.

"What an irony," thought Tom. However, Tom didn't contest the charges and the divorce was granted, ending a three-and-half years' marriage of a domineering and scheming wife and a hard-working and forgiveful husband whose every good move and achievement was recklessly shared with his lesbian wife and his first and only shortcoming – financial crisis – could not be tolerated by his blood-sucking wife.

Tom had met Kate in the day trading firm where he was trading and Kate worked. It was in the dawn of Tom's love with his new self, new principles and financial success. He'd developed a prowess for stock picking and analysis and it always worked for him. In his one year of trading in the firm, Tom had not lost a cent. Kate watched him grow rich and richer by the day as his expertise in stock picking flourished. Tom became even more attractive the day he cleared £400,000 at the end of a day's trading. Kate beamed with smiles whenever she was near Tom and each time Tom looked her way. The next day, Kate ambushed him. She approached Tom as he came out of the elevator to the parking lot, falling in step with him.

"Congratulations on your impressive spread yesterday. It's the highest spread I've witnessed in my eight months in the firm. I love your stock picking ability. I wish you could give a friend, I mean a Well Wisher, a tenth of the attention you give your stocks. Yours must be a very lucky woman," said Kate, beaming.

"Thanks," Tom had replied. "But I'm flattered. I wish I had a woman," he added.

"You mean you're . . ." said Kate, knitting her brows quizzically. She'd broken the ice and got to the point of her interest.

"Yes, I'm single and free," Tom.

"Or, women are blind or you don't give them the chance, and you ain't gay of course," Kate probed coyly.

"It's none of the above. No woman has ever wanted me," said Tom sincerely.

"Except one, one you never cared to notice. A simple attention could get the two of you happy," said Kate.

"If only I knew the one," replied Tom.

"And if only you pay attention, you will know her. The one is always there from the beginning and she is with you and she is . . . ? You answer it, Tom," said Kate.

"Ehmm," hemmed Tom, smiling. "And the one is you," he said finally.

"Me?" said Kate coyly.

Tom is enjoying the indulgence.

"You said so," Kate said, happy that Tom rose to the

bait.

"I must hurry, see you tomorrow," said Kate as she turned and left.

Tom watched as she walked towards the elevator.

"See you tomorrow," he said out loud as she disappeared into the elevator.

CHAPTER 12
Moscow, Russia

Tom and Kate got married six months later. Life was good and smooth for the couple and Tom's day trading enterprise flourished. They were a happy family, or so it seemed, until Tom traded a large volume of entertainment stock – the Manchester United football club stock. Tom traded an enormous volume of the stock assisted by the credit from the brokers. The day trading firm lent him over two hundred percent more than the value of the securities he purchased against the fifty percent authorized limit. But lending limits is not what borders the brokers whose interest is getting the client to trade as many securities as possible and pay them commission. Tom in his prudence had studied the stock's profile before trading the stocks.

Manchester United Football Club has just won the English Premier League Championships, and they will play the finals of the European Club Side Championship. The club has just contracted the world's FIFA acclaimed best player from Brazil and the world's number three best player, a nineteen year old mid fielder from Algeria. The two will resume in the club after the finals of the Euro Club Side Championship. The present coach of the club is going into retirement after a beribboned career and will hand over the coaching job to Mr. Cromwell, the world's best coach with three World Cups to his record, two European Cups of Nations, and great leadership prowess. All seemed in order, hedged and contained even at possible uncertainties when Tom clicked the mouse highlighting his quote and confirmed. He was ready to hold the stock not just for hours as usual but for holds – buy and hold, to maximize profit, but little did he know about the man called Bradley, his problems, ambitions and how he was bent on resolving them – his plot.

While Tom analyzed the MAN UTD stock, Bradley was solving the puzzles in the plot. Hardly a day passes without Bradley putting a call through to the Beltov Hotel in the Lefortovo district of Moscow where Betsky, his Russian wife, has been lodging for the past one month on her "save-his-soul" draft dodge mission. The Chechnya rebels of Georgia were warming up for war against Moscow, and their leader, Dzokhar Dudayev, has vowed not to negotiate with Moscow and has sworn to win the war at any cost. The rumour was circulating rapidly that the Chechnya rebels have acquired a good measure of tons of genetically enhanced anthrax bacteria from the Sverdlonsk city stockpile of biological weapons in a laboratory of the communist Soviet legacy, and have vowed to use the deadly pink powder if necessary to win the war. It has caused a great concern to many parents who have draft age children. The Russian military camps, where draftees on their two-year compulsory military service are enrolled and sent to war six months after learning to fire a weapon will soon be teeming with boys of eighteen to twenty-seven years. Betsky's son will turn twenty years in the following months. There was no doubt he would be drafted to fight for Russia.

Betsky met her ex-husband, the father of her only son, Koytov, in the balcony of his house in Moscow. If

Daniskov was delighted to see her, he didn't betray it. He listened attentively as Betsky told her request, his face expressionless.

"You have always been a capitalist," was Daniskov's first statement when Betsky finished telling him what spanked her back to Moscow.

"I know you have never been a Communist. You hated the Soviet power. But you love Moscow and who loves Moscow loves Russia because Moscow is the heart of Russia. If it had been the Afghan war, I would've easily seen your reasons. But now, it's Russia, a capitalist Russia. Why not defend the Russian territory, especially now that atheism is gone. These days it's different, the soldiers have Orthodox Church priests with them in the camps and fronts. The priests pray for them before they go to the war fronts to raise their fighting spirits and the priests explains to them how much heaven gratifies a brave soldier and bless the spirits of the fallen soldiers, just like the western style. I don't see why one must dodge draft now that God is with the Russian military," said Daniskov.

"Your request is suicidal. My wife is with me today because of the children. Our marriage has not been so smooth. Two years into our marriage, when she was in her first pregnancy, I had the accident and that earned me this wheelchair," said Daniskov, looking down at the wheels of his chair.

"As you very well know, my pension is meagre. If I must suggest divorce to my wife, she will accept it. It will be a good riddance for her. But it's like telling me to jump off a one-thousand metre high cliff."

Silence.

"Let Koytov go to war and serve the Motherland," said Daniskov. "You have no good enough reason to stop him from serving his Motherland," he added.

"I've got pretty good reasons but if you don't reason with me you won't understand," began Betsky. "Dan, we ain't talking of me and you, nor are we talking of the lost Soviet units in the Taliban forest of Afghanistan from the Afghan war or the luck the survivors had, not even the consequences of the war on the health of the soldiers, or the fate of a maimed Russian soldier and his family.

"Dan, I'm talking of my only child, your child, our child, I'm talking of the Islamic rebels of the Chechnya mountains and what they will do to make their secession a success – their desperation.

"Why push Koytov to war when you can save him. I've no other child. You've got two others with your present wife. If you love your child, Koytov, so much as you proved in the custody case, why send him to war?" said Betsky.

"I've never seen a more unpatriotic Russian. You ran away to the west. Now you forget that the west built their heaven with the power of arms and with a strengthened military. Now you come with this western brash confidence and tell me to divorce my new wife so that he will not go to war, so that we prove he is the only grown-up left to take care of his crippled father.

"What a blatant nonpatriot you are.

"I'm not against those who emigrated to the west and went native in London, England. Immigration is indigenous to man and life, but sabotage against the Motherland is unpardonable. In the west, youths are often proud to defend their land in war, whether it is in Vietnam, in Iraq, Falklands, or in Afghanistan.

"Brainwashed!" said Daniskov.

A pause.

"Let's be considerate to the young man, Koytov,"

said Betsky.

"If you are this considerate, why separate me from my wife when I'm on the wheelchair with a meagre pension?" said Daniskov.

"Because that is a very good reason for him to dodge the draft. It will be alleged that he is there to take care of you, since your other children are minors and will stay with their mother. Besides, I'm not separating you from your wife forever. It is only for as long as the war lasts. As for your meagre pension, things will be fixed to that effect," said Betsky.

"Things will be fixed to that effect?" asked Dan.

"Yes," said Betsky.

"What?" asked Daniskov.

"You tell me," said Betsky. "What floats your boat?" added Betsky.

"You want to buy me over? You capitalist, my conscience is not for sale," replied Daniskov.

Betsky opened her mouth to talk but restrained. She recalled that Daniskov is a very proud man and wished she had said it in a more subtle and acceptable manner.

"No, I'm not nobling you, I only mean we, every

member of the family could come together and see to it," said Betsky.

"Nobody is coming together with you. I hate capitalism. You are the only capitalist in the family and if you think you can fix it then fix it alone.

"A quarter of a million dollars can fix it, now fix it, lady fixer," said Dan mockingly.

"A quarter?" Betsky said, surprised that Dan would be saying such an enormous sum of money and that he would be talking about the safety and life of their child in terms of money, American dollars.

"Yes, a quarter. Nerhcy will like it, she will be happy and sure that I'm financially afloat as she leaves me," said Daniskov.

Betsky's shining eyes looked him over, burning with hate, but she knew she had to take it easy. Daniskov was the only remaining pivot to the success of her mission. Her son doesn't have enough educational qualification to be enrolled in any accredited institution of higher learning which could afford him the opportunity of being drafted on an officer's track – a non-combatant post, or the draft could be deferred indefinitely as long as he stays enrolled in the institution until he turns 27 years, the age limit for drafting.

Adoption for draft age men has been barred until after the war, otherwise she would've walked into any orphanage and adopted any baby that was under the age of three. As a single father of a minor under three years, he would get an automatic exemption.

The popular medical deferment has been subjected to random cross-checking scrutiny by the Kremlin medical squad. It had recently brought more danger and problems to the youths who are treated as conscripts when their medical alibis were revoked.

Betsky was laying on her hotel room bed, smarting over the insult from her former husband, Daniskov, for equating the life of her son to a quarter of a million dollars when the phone trilled off on the bedside table. She stretched and picked the receiver.

"Hello, gorgeous," came Bradley's voice. "I bet it went well with your ex?"

"Not at all," Betsky replied.

"How do you mean?"

"He wasn't a bit savvy over the reality. He mocked me out of his house. It will only be fixed with a quarter of a million dollars, he told me," said Betsky.

A pause.

"Hello?" said Betsky.

"I'm here. A quarter of a million dollars?" asked Bradley, his mind racing, trying to thrash out a plan, adding and subtracting on how and where such an amount could be scratched out.

"That's a tidy sum, but his life and Betsky's happiness is worth a lot more than that. There is still time. Let's see what we can do," said Bradley.

CHAPTER 13

All day and night long, Bradley pondered the prospect of Betsky becoming childless just because they couldn't rally some $250,000 to fix a divorce so that he could dodge the draft. He knew how it felt to lose a son, especially because of financial shortcomings. He had lost a South Korean son in the early 80's when he was working with a Swiss pharmaceutical company. He'd gone to Seoul, South Korea, in search of the so-called true variety of ginseng, its optimum cultivation rules. Ginseng is an oddly shaped root that contains many compounds with variety of medical powers ranging from stimulants to tranquilizers.

Shingu-xi, a childless widow, runs a bar a few blocks from the hotel where Bradley was lodging.

Bradley caroused in the bar in the evenings. The bar teemed with a bevy of flirty fine teenage girls from Burma, Thailand, and rural towns of South Korea. The girls flirted with customers of the bar, getting them to empty their wallets on drinks while they earn commissions. Bradley met Tansuga – a young Burmese girl with whom he enjoyed and spent his evenings in the bar. Shangu-xi has always billed him for champagne while Tansuga sipped cheap spirits. She finds it's an appropriate revenge, her own little way of inflicting hurt on the western imperialists. One night Bradley had gone to a nightclub in central Seoul, the night was still young and people had not started getting drunk. The dancing floor was teeming as a spirit-lifting music blasts from the speakers. Bradley looked into the crowd on the dancing floor and somewhere in the centre of the hall is a familiar face, a lady in her thirties. He was unable to really place the face at that moment, but he shouldered his way through the crowd to the lady. The lady seemed not to recognize him at first. They danced the number together and when the music was over they took a table together and ordered some drinks. They drank and got tipsy as the night aged and people began to leave for their respective homes. Shangu-xi offered to drive Bradley home and he accepted. It was a fifteen minute drive to his hotel. Bradley invited Shangu-xi in for more drinks and she obliged. They had few more glasses of drink and spent the rest of the night together. Bradley made love to her all night long and he knew his stuff when it comes to sex. To Shangu-xi, who has not had sex in a dozen months, it was an enthralling experience, a night that will forever excite her memory.

Bradley went to the bar two nights later and Shangu-xi met him in the doorway, embraced and kissed him on the lips. She led Bradley to the VIP corner of the bar and went to mix them drinks. Tansuga was in the ladies' when Bradley entered. Coming back into the bar, she saw Bradley and walked up to him and sat beside him and began teasing him as usual. When Shangu-xi came back with two glasses of drink, Tansuga thought it was for them and stretched to pick a glass but Shangu-xi drew back, placed the drinks on the table, and quietly pushed of Tansuga's right arm that was resting on Bradley's shoulders and ordered her out of the bar. For the rest of Bradley's stay in Seoul, she kept him within eyesight and warded off any potential adversary.

Shangu-xi, whose dead husband was a ginseng grower and trader, lectured Bradley on all she knew about ginseng root. When Bradley left Seoul he promised Shangu-xi he would be coming back to Seoul in nine months to see her. Shangu-xi was two months pregnant but Bradley didn't know. When Bradley came back to Seoul nine months later, Shangu-xi presented him with a baby boy.

"This is your boy," she told Bradley, who stood agape.

He never liked the surprise, but nonetheless he accepted the paternity of the child and called him Seouly. He stayed five months in Seoul before going back to the United States of America.

CHAPTER 14
Bridgewater, New York

It was another nine months before Bradley saw Shan-gu-xi and his son, Seouly, again. He'd invited them to spend the summer with him in his native town of Bridgewater sixty-five kilometres west of New York City. Two months into their stay in Bridgewater, Seouly developed some troubling symptoms. He lost the ability to turn his neck properly and found it difficult to raise his arms. He choked regularly during feeding, shook, and his reflexes were very slow. Bradley and Shangu-xi took their infant child to a paediatrician who assured them the child was all right but promised to have a thorough laboratory test of his situation. A week later, Bradley and Shangu-xi were told that Seouly was suffering from a rare muscular disorder, which as yet had no cure except for experimental treatment in the teaching hospitals.

At the New York University Medical Centre, Bradley was told that in the absence of a company investing in research and development programme in which their child would be admitted as a volunteer and receive free treatment, he had to spend over $1 million. Bradley didn't have that kind of money and his health insurance didn't cover such rare treatments.

"The disease is a rare disease classified as an orphan disease, one of the five thousand rare disorders, so rare that drug companies do not invest in developing the drugs for its cure as they won't make enough profits or even have their investment capital back cause there will be too few clients," the doctor told Bradley and Shangu-xi.

Bradley took his son home and in company of Shan-gu-xi, nursed his son, hoping on a miracle for his cure. But one evening after they had dinner, Bradley was holding Seouly in his arms when Seouly began shaking and his breath choked.

"Papa! Papa!" he called out to Bradley.

"Yes," Bradley replied. "Daddy is here, Seouly, daddy loves you, son."

But Seouly's eyes rolled wildly, he stiffened and died.

Bradley buried Seouly, the only child that had called him father. He lost this child for the lack of drugs and funds.

Shangu-xi went back to Seoul, broken-hearted, and Bradley moved to London, England.

CHAPTER 15

The death of his son in his arms has always been vivid in his memory. And he never wants the whole world to become ill with the rare disease that killed his son before the research and development of the drug of cure would be embarked on.

Over the years, Bradley spent as much money and time as he could in the laboratory researching the disease, its cause and cure. He discovered that the disease is caused by the lack of an essential enzyme whose replacement could cure the victims of the disease. He also found out that other diseases present symptoms similar to those presented by the rare disease. Mercury poisoning presents symptoms that include shaking, stumbling, slow reflexes, reduced coordination, poor vision and eventually death. And Bradley knew that mercury collects in the fatty tissues of the fish that people eat, collecting in the form of methyl mercury which is fat soluble.

Methyl mercury accumulates more in large predatory fishes like shark and swordfish. Bradley studied the new pronouncement from the Agency of Toxic Substances and Disease Registry – a part of the Centres for Disease Control and Prevention. The agency had pronounced that it was safe to consume 0.5 micrograms of mercury per kilogram of body weight per day. He reached that anything around 0.9 micrograms to 1 microgram per kilogram of body weight will prompt mercury poisoning. He knew that an enzyme, which is capable of stopping slow reflexes, shaking and poor coordination in the rare disease could as well stop them in mercury poisoning.

Shark and swordfish are on the top list of major dietary source of methyl mercury to humans. It will take a tidy sum to start a shark and swordfish pond large enough to supply half the English population, Europe and export to the USA. Bradley hadn't got any money. He'd had to struggle and save so much to carry out his research in his private laboratory.

Bradley is now forming an investing philosophy, which includes the stressful act of creating ways of sickening and curing people. He knew that it would be better and more easily done in Africa, Asia, and South American countries where controls for toxic substances in the food chain is lax. But the problem is, if he gets millions of people sick in Africa, the disease may still be an orphan disease in the western nations because nobody may have the money to buy the drug that would be subsequently developed and his aim will be defeated. If the disease were infectious, especially sexually transmitted, he would introduce it into the African, Asian and South American population and then wait for some time for Europeans and North Americans on sex tours to Africa and Asia to contract it and then introduce it into the western population, but alas. . . .

He then decided to start a shark and swordfish pond where he would breed them alongside other species with an excess of methyl mercury in the pond water.

CHAPTER 16

By the next morning, Bradley's investing philosophy had grown to include short selling of stocks. On the piece of paper before him was a list of companies whose stocks are listed with the London stock exchange. He asterisked two companies, both were entertainment stocks – the MAN UTD stock and the PZ rugby team stock. To choose between the two, he tossed a 20p coin, choosing the obverse side of the coin for the MAN UTD stock and the reverse side for the PZ rugby stock. The coin landed on the study table with the obverse side up.

"The MAN UTD stock will take the heat," he murmured, and totally decided to take the plunge.

He would need the services of the Mob to get his plot through. At the thought of the Mob, Johnny Bandit came to mind immediately. Johnny Bandit was the don of the London Brixton Mob. The next day, he was in Johnny's place. He failed, or rather wasn't allowed to, see Johnny himself and he refused to speak with the Mob's lieutenant commander, Comrade Harvey.

A week later, at Johnny Bandit's place, Bradley filled in the visitor's form presented to him by the gateman and was allowed passage into the compound. After a well-detailed body search, he was led into an office some five meters down the wide corridor away from the office he was taken into a week earlier. Bradley was ushered to a two-seater cushion. The office was as lavishly furnished and ostentatious as a gangster's office could be, overly intimidating. He waited for another five minutes, aware that somebody was watching him on a screen somewhere, before a man who looked in his late forties with a great aura of self assurance and flair strutted towards him from behind the blinders that moved slowly sideways to clear his way. As he approached, Bradley stood up and kept his eyes steady on his face, not moving them up and down so that the man wouldn't feel like he was being sized up. He offered his hand for shake with a broad show of the teeth.

"I'm Bandit," he said. "Johnny Bandit," he added.

"Bradley," he replied, taking his hand, aware that he was in the presence of the most dangerous man in the United Kingdom, the revered Johnny Bandit. He, Bradley, could be cut into pieces and thrown to the pigs or dissolved in a drum of corrosive acid by Johnny's men at the wave of a finger.

Johnny's personal charm and warmth is electrifying, something definitely not known to the public. He doesn't in the least look like a mobster as Bradley had envisaged. Johnny took his seat and crossed his legs.

"So?" he said with a nod of his head.

"Ehem," Bradley started but hesitated, not knowing if he was to talk.

"Come on, go on, tell me what happened that you want to see Johnny Bandit himself," said Johnny.

"I need the services of the Mob," Bradley said.

"So how can we help you?"

Bradley started, but hesitated, his eyes moved sideways as if he was searching for any trouble or faults in his plot, but satisfied he steadied. He's done his homework very well: the Brixton Mob have no shares with the MAN UTD stock, unless they do have some holdings in a false name, but in that case he would feign ignorance. Bradley went ahead and explained his quest to Johnny in minute detail.

"Why maim, why not kill, and all the three of them?" Johnny asked when Bradley finished. Johnny had been a MAN UTD fan since childhood, but this was strictly business.

"Because maiming them will serve our purpose better," replied Bradley.

"And what is your exact purpose?" asked Johnny.

"I'm sorry, ehem . . ." Bradley fumbled.

"Intruding, eh?" said Bandit. "But the family never sign a contract of this sort. It appears very simple but actually very difficult, and interesting though. Besides, with the family nothing is intrusion. To maim the world's best soccer player, the world's highest paid soccer player and Europe's best and most celebrated coach must be a big business, there must be money to be made, and the family wouldn't mind joining as a partner and not just a mercenary," said Johnny Bandit.

A pause as the two men studied themselves. There is something in the angular facial curves and lines of Mr. Bandit that Bradley couldn't read nor trust, but nevertheless he was happy that Mr. Bandit rose to his bait.

"Quite in order, just as I want it, I have no money to pay the Mob upfront," thought Mr. Bradley but not betraying his delight.

"But Johnny . . ." Bradley started, a light frown creasing his temple, a frown of discordance, but he was only acting.

"No, don't Johnny me," retorted Johnny Bandit. "You have been here on two different occasions insisting to see me in person, you never trusted my lieutenants enough, not even the family commander, and now you don't trust me or you're pretending not to.

"Look, you are not here to ask me for justice as I had imagined, you are here to plead with Johnny Bandit and family to maim good people, who work honestly for their living, one of the most loved people in the United Kingdom, Europe and around the global village. To hamstring the careers of young people who, with their talents, have been adding some colour to the world of sports, livening it up, and have been a source of adrenaline to many people around the world.

So tell me now, why must they be put out of business, off their career for good?" said Johnny.

"Okay, between me and you," Bradley said.

"No, between me, you and the rest of the Mob officers."

"Between me and you?" Bradley repeated, more in confusion than insistence.

Johnny Bandit breathed deeply in and looked away to hide the irritation in his eyes, lest he frighten him.

"You have a lot of courage mister. Who are you?" he said, turning to face Bradley.

"I'm Bradley, an American biotechnologist," said Bradley.

"Yes, go on, more about yourself," said Johnny.

"Well, after graduating from a college in New York USA in 1940, I spent time pirating bio-species from around the world for biotech companies and pharmaceutical industries. When the war started, I joined the western army and fought the German troops in France. After the war, I joined the Jewish Joint Distribution Committee, helping the Jewish survivors of the war. My most esteemed task in the Committee includes organizing the secret exodus of the Jews to the nascent state of Israel until the route we were plying then was uncovered and blocked by the Communists, who feared that the Committee was an object of the western imperialists and Zionists to spy on and infiltrate the Bolshevik regimes. It was like coming to the Red Sea but we had no Moses, no walking stick and nobody struck the sea three times to make way for us. So we were trapped.

In the fifties, I left the organization and went on a bio-specimen collection in the African continent, but rejoined the Committee again in the sixties when I negotiated yet another secret exodus of North African Jews to Israel. This time sympathetic regimes of governments of neutral countries gave us cover and support, to disguise the destination of our Jewish guests. Just like the nations that sympathized with the Biblical Israel during their exodus from Egypt to the Promised Land. During this period, I went to Romania with some Committee members to help negotiate with the then Romanian Communist leader, Nicolae Ceausescu for the release of the Romanian Jews.

Nicolae Ceausescu was an obstinate man, negotiating with him was like negotiating with the then Egyptian Pharaohs, but this time the plague wasn't needed to get him to soft pedal."

"Nicolae Ceausescu?" asked Johnny Bandit, frowning in concentration.

"Yes Nicolae, the dictator who was killed with his wife, Elena, after the 1989 anti-Communist revolt in Romania."

"Yeah! Yeah!" said Johnny, nodding in concordance.

"After that, I left the Committee again, satisfied that I had helped the Jews enough. I went back to bio-specimen collection from around the globe. When I retired, I went into research and development of drugs. Until seven days ago I was a full-time private researcher and today I am a private researcher turned investor," said Bradley crisply, sure that he impressed him at least with the war thing and the Jewish story, though it was all lies. Bradley had been a biopirate all his life. It was only a stunt to capture Johnny's attention and respect. After all, it was in vogue to be a World War II veteran soldier and to be pro-Semitism. Besides, Bradley had heard how much Johnny loves the Jews, and that Johnny Bandit's Brixton Mob lawyer, the man whose legal expertise keeps Johnny and the Mob members on the streets, is a Jew. Also, the woman Johnny loves is a Jewish lady, an actress who refused to marry him, not wanting the glamour and popularity of being Johnny Bandit's wife.

"That's an alpha profile you've got," said Johnny, a timbre of respect in his voice. "You are now an investor, eh?" asked Johnny.

"I see," he added, nodding understandingly.

"So what about the MAN UTD goal getters and the coach? Anything to do with your investments?" asked Johnny.

"Yes, I'm starting my investment with them," said Bradley.

"By maiming them?" probed Johnny.

"Yes," replied Bradley.

"How?" he asked, getting up.

For a moment, Bradley was afraid.

Johnny walked over to the plush bar at the far end of the large airy office room. He mixed them drinks in two glasses and came back and handed Bradley one glass and sipped his as he sat down and waited for Bradley's response.

Bradley sipped his and sat upright, adjusting himself in the seat.

"You see," Bradley started, "I've borrowed enormous volume of the MAN UTD stocks at its three-digit share price and I'm hoping to short-sell the stock, or rather return them at a lower price than I borrowed them," said Bradley.

"What do you mean by short sell?" asked Johnny. "Is it the so-called Parando's paradox that I recently heard of?" he added.

"No, it isn't Parando's paradox. In Parando's paradox one wouldn't need to hedge one's investment with the nose of the guns and the blades of the scalpel. All one needs to do is find a losing stock, make an alternate investment, and then make your profit. It's liquefying the mechanical properties of ratchets. A ratchet with its saw-tooth shape allows movement in one direction but hinders it in the alternate direction. You know stuff like that, but this is not it. This is short selling. I borrowed the stock and I'm hoping that the share prices of the stock will fall and if it falls the difference between the price at which I borrowed them and the price of the share at the time I return or deliver them to a buyer is called the 'Spread', and that's my profit, but if the share price of the stock rises, that's if the stock appreciates in value, then I have to return the stocks at a higher price than I borrowed them and the difference between the borrow price and the delivery price is the spread I will lose. In this case, I will bleed money into the stock, so to hedge this investment, I've come here today to speak with the Mob and ask for help."

"So how will maiming the two players and the coach help the spread?" asked Johnny.

"The two players and the coach and of course the performance of the team in the recent times; the matches they won, the finals they will play and the trophy they will take home, but especially the two players and the coach are responsible for the market value, the stock bubble of the MAN UTD stocks. Blowing off the kneecaps of the players, hamstringing them and blinding the coach will burst the bubble. I mean crumble the elevated share price of the stock," said Bradley.

"And if you leave them?" asked Johnny Bandit.

"The bubble grows larger and my loss grows with it," replied Bradley.

"Why blind the coach? Why not hamstring him like the players?" asked Johnny.

"Because he is so good, he can win the World Cup or any trophy for that matter from a wheel chair," replied Bradley.

Johnny was silent, his gaze distant.

"I like it," he said finally. "It is a sophisticated corporate technique, robbery though," he added. "So that's why you're here? What's in it for the Mob?"

"You tell me," replied Bradley.

"How much are we making on the deal?" asked Johnny.

"Not specific," Bradley replied.

"How do you mean?" Johnny said, crisply and alert.

"It depends on the spread, I mean the level to which the stock depreciates. If the spread is large, then the profit is large. But I bet we make a minimum of £4m," Bradley explained.

"Half the spread for me," said Johnny.

"And half the spread for me," enjoined Bradley.

"This is not a greedy man," thought Bradley.

Johnny stood up from his chair and started towards Bradley, who stood up and they clinked their half empty glasses.

"Half the spread for each," they said in tandem and emptied their glasses in one gulp.

Bradley was very happy because he had no money to pay the advance payment to the Mob and even more pleased that it was Johnny who suggested the settlement. Now he has nothing to invest and risk. If things go wrong and the share prices rise, but with the Mob nothing goes wrong when the theme is destruction, they always get it right, there is nothing to worry about.

"Any time limit for the execution?" asked Johnny.

"Not necessarily," Bradley said. "But within three weeks will be optimum. It will allow us to take advantage of the market bubble. The share price of the stock will peak by next week. That will give a very large sum in spread. Four weeks is a good time frame," said Bradley.

CHAPTER 17

Mr. Edward is the Mob private detective, an ex-Scotland Yard detective dismissed from the Police force for premeditated false submission on a high profile criminal case involving Johnny Bandit. A case that was the closest the Scotland Yard has got to putting Johnny Bandit behind bars. Edward has no doubt about the urgency his findings on the daily habit of the three, the best, the highest and the coach, as he received the mobilization vouchers from the Mob treasurer. Five days of intensive investigation revealed all he needed to know about the "best" as the South American footballer is now referred to in the Mob crowd and the coach, but the habits of the "highest" as the Algerian player is tagged is yet to be deciphered, because he is a loner.

The "best" will be going down to his native Brazilian beach city of Rio de Janeiro for the annual Carnival festival in the next two weeks. When not in the training camp, the coach is an opera addict. He's never missed an opera concert in the Covent Garden. From all indications, the highest is always in the house when not in the training camp. He drives straight home after every training session, but under tight security. But how he spends his day in the home is still an enigma to Edward.

Edward was gazing at the TV, imagining how to make up the book on the "highest's" indoors profile before submitting it the next morning. The talk show programme was back to the screen after a short commercial. The screen blinked and there was the wife of the world's highest paid footballer granting interview to the talk show host.

"He likes relaxing in my bedroom during his two hours afternoon nap, after his usual 10-12 noon Sunday morning exercise. He wakes up at 9:00 a.m. every Sunday morning and starts his exercise at 10:00 a.m. While he exercises and eventually goes to sleep, I use the time to visit friends and relations in the company of my driver and my bodyguard. I make sure I go back home at thereabout 2:00 p.m. 'cause he will need my company when he wakes up. He is such a lovely baby. I'm very lucky and I'm in love," she said frankly, looking immensely pleased with life.

Edward smiled and made up his dossier.

At first it seemed fettering that the "best" will be going to Rio the next two weeks, but on closer examination, the Mob top rankers reached that it is very good because in Rio de Janeiro he will be with his native folks, there will be no tight round the clock sophisticated English security as is obtained here in London.

In Brazil, the poor mix with the rich, there isn't much exclusivity, he will be most relaxed and the job easier to execute. The Carnival is so well celebrated in Rio de Janeiro that everybody will be carried away by the festive atmospherics. Besides, if things go wrong and the Mob's hit man escapes the anger of the local population the court will charge him for bodily injury and the sentence will be in the neighbourhood of one year in a semi-open prison where he goes to work, community service, in the city during the day and only comes to sleep in the prison yard at nights. That wouldn't be so bad, a one-year repose in Rio de Janeiro, with paid accommodation, feeding, security and lots of sun. And at the worst-case scenario, he gets a very long sentence. It will be very easy to arrange for an escape from the yards. Once he is in London, he is safe. England has no extradition treaty with Brazil.

* * *

Rio de Janeiro, Brazil

David was chosen for the Rio de Janeiro mission. He was given a crash Portuguese language course. It was his first international gangster mission but, armed with the city map, weather conditions and address of his victim, money, and a sunny disposition, he was ready to top the challenge. Dave could see the outline of the city of Rio de Janeiro through the side window of the aircraft as it descended and circulated before landing on the runway of the Galeon Rio International Airport. He'd never seen a more beautiful landscape. A city formed on the edges of the Atlantic Ocean, with three beaches right inside the city. He didn't miss the city's most conspicuous symbol of Christianity and welcome, the giant statue of Christ as it stands with hands wide spread atop the Corcovado Mountain. The Rio city air was humid and smelly. Dave took a taxi to the Copacabana borough of Rio city and checked into a hotel at Avenida Atlantico. A bellhop collected the key to his room and led him into an elevator where he got his first pump of adrenaline. As the elevator operator, a balding middle aged man that looked more like an unfortunate actuary than a lazy elevator-sitter kissed the Madonna he was holding in his left palm and crossed himself with the right hand before closing the elevator door. Dave was afraid because elevator falls are common in developing nations and the elevator was fairly old. As the elevator started on its ascent to the tenth floor of the hotel, Dave braced his hands against the wall of the elevator as though they were brakes, to stop it from falling. The room was large, airy, and overlooking the Copacabana beach and was constantly freshened by the cool breeze from the nearby beach. Dave spent the rest of the day sleeping. In the evening, he walked down the avenue of his hotel and ended up sitting in one of the roadside open bars with plastic seats and tables set outside in the open air. The next morning he hired a car from a car rentals depot in the street adjacent to his hotel avenue, and toured the Copacabana district and beyond. At first, driving was very odd because he was used to the right hand drive and the keep left traffic rules of England, but after about five hours of driving, he became adjusted to the left hand drive and keep right traffic system of Rio de Janeiro. He had never seen a city in such a merry and festive mood nor had he ever seen such a large crowd of half-naked beautiful women in the streets of one city alone. Nakedness, obscenity, merrymaking, fist fighting and drunkenness seemed to be part of the city's daily life.

Dave went back to his hotel at 2:00 p.m. that day and collected his key from the receptionist. On opening his room door, he was greeted by the stale overnight air of an unmade hotel room. He swept across the room to the telephone that was sitting fallow on the table, to call the management and complain of the room's untidiness, but restrained himself and replaced the receiver on its cradle. Complaining was the easiest way to get noticed in this fifteen-floor high hotel, the thing Dave least wanted. So he accepted their lax dirty manner and kept quiet.

In his first effort for his mission in Rio de Janeiro,

Dave visited Barra de Tijuca, a district for the newly monied and social climbers. It is in this borough that the "best" is said to have his mansion. Dave drove past the beautiful ridges of mountains that demarcate the district of Barra de Tijuca from the rest of the city of Rio, until he came to the sign post that welcomes would-be visitors.

"Smile 'cause you are in the Barra de Tijuca".

In the Barra district, Dave immediately realised that he had to change his scripted plan of execution. The plan had been to kidnap the "best" while he strolls his neighbourhood as he does in England under tight security and take him to a safe place where the hamstringing would be done. But here there are no sidewalks and one can only go around from one part of the district to the other by car. There are none of the open corner bars that Rio and Brazil are generally known for. It is so different a neighbourhood that it might complicate his mission. But as a professional, he had to figure out another viable plot. He contemplated calling England to complain about his findings in the Barra district, but restrained, because, he was strictly instructed not to call home except to notify the Mob of the hotel room number he is occupying, and the Mob already had this information, so he mustn't call them again except if he was in danger and needed any kind of help or reinforcement. He was not in any danger nor did he need any urgent help, it was only a change in the plot, and he could go solo about it. Dave slowed down as he drove past "best's" mansion. The house had about fifty metres front lawn planted with trees and flowers asymmetrically arranged. A uniformed policeman and one plain cloth security man were manning the entrance gate.

Dave left Barra de Tijuca and headed for Rochinha, a ghetto district where the "best" was born and brought up. From the top of the Rochinha ghetto mountains, or morro de Rochinha as it is locally called, one can have a panoramic view of Barra de Tijuca and its relatively heavenly setting. Dave parked his car on the hard shoulder of a not-too-busy street and decided to tour the Rochinha district on foot. After four hours of touring the streets of Rochinha, he came back to the street where his car was parked. As he approached the car, he saw two dirty looking boys, obviously street boys, making away with the car stereo. They had picked the car door.

"Much better than breaking the car side glasses", thought Dave.

Dave tried to chase after them at first, a normal instinct and reaction from someone whose property is being stolen, but hesitated. The shopkeeper from whose shop Dave had bought a pack of Hollywood cigarettes earlier was faster and chased after them.

"Ladrao! Ladrao!" he shouted.

"Thief! Thief!" Dave thought in an attempt to interpret what the shopkeeper was shouting. Dave was right with his interpretation.

A police patrol vehicle coincidentally was approaching from the opposite direction, towards the fleeing boys. Two other people had joined the shopkeeper in the chase now. Dave saw a policeman jump down from the patrol vehicle, aimed at the fleeing preteenage boys and spewed bullets at them from his semi-automatic police gun, as their pursuers dived for safety. The boys fell face down onto the ground, wriggling in pain, and died minutes afterward. The policeman walked up to them and aimed at their heads, shooting two times at each. He bent down and picked the car stereo and beckoned to one of the pursuers and gave it to him. One other policeman came down from the jeep to help lift the corpses onto the police jeep. The shop owner came to Dave, who was leaning against the car to give him the blood stained car stereo.

"Here is your stereo, cidadao" said the shop owner.

Dave shook his head in refusal.

"It's yours, take it," insisted the shop owner.

Dave noticed the anger in his eyes.

"Take it for yourself," he spluttered.

"Para me?" asked the shop owner.

"Yes," said Dave.

"Obrigado," he said, turned and crossed the street into his shop.

As Dave drove down the sloppy exit roads of the ghetto, he felt bad for the reckless killing of the two street boys for mere car stereo theft and his own for that matter.

Despite its apparent natural beautiful landscape, beaches, sun, sex, and . . . Rio is a very violent city.

How can a city and district as Rochinha breed a talented child like "best" for the wonders and deceptions of fame and riches?

"Compared with the neighbourhood I grew up in

London, England, this is a jungle, a true hell," thought Dave.

Dave tried to picture the "best" in his preteen years playing soccer with his peer group, barefooted in the dusty fields. But he couldn't piece and reconcile him in the picture. "Best" is too rich, too famous today for Dave to appropriately imagine his urchin background. His poor family background, the early part of his life, when the dream, the vision of the outlines and grandeur of another brand of life based on his talent, his ability to make fans cry in delight and joy. Tears of joy and delight that must've streaked down his own cheeks during the formative part of his life, because in a football country like Brazil, with lots of football mega-idols, someone must have inspired him. And using personal will and determination, he'd empowered the ambition, the dream to come true. He felt some pain for him for what he was going to do to him. The injury, the pain he will inflict and cause him, ending his career gruesomely, a career he had dreamt and toiled for all his life. And ironically he, Dave, doesn't know and may never know why he's come thousands of kilometres from London across the Atlantic to South America to knock off his knee cap and cut off his hamstrings. It is even more dangerous a job to do than killing because he must get close enough to him to overpower, kidnap and then do the job. If it were an outright killing, it would have been an easier job because he could do it from a fifty metre distance.

Could it be a war for positions in the football pitch among the players of MAN UTD and rival football clubs that he's come here to maim him or could it be envy? Could it be for a gambling bet? Or probably it is part of being at the top where the tendency is to be knocked off. However, whatever it is, he is a professional hit man, not an investigator, thank goodness he is not a football fanatic. He likes and enjoys football, but not a fanatic: otherwise he would find the job a bit more difficult for sentimental reasons because whoever loves football is obviously bound to love the "best". He is one of the players that make this brand of entertainment worth watching and wasting one's time on.

A pause.

He remembered and extolled the dictum of "Uncle" as the Mob commander is referred to in the Mob par-lance:

"In crime there are no sentiments, no conscience, no remorse, the more barbaric the better. Often use your head not your heart. Always be a professional," Uncle always told them.

David is a professional and had never felt compassion for his would-be victims, just as he had never felt fear in his whole life, except for the moment while he was in the flight from London to Rio de Janeiro.

He felt fear because. . .

He didn't risk nine hours of turbulent flight from London to Rio to feel compassion for the victim, but to execute the Mob's order to the letters, otherwise he the hunter would turn to be the hunted.

. . . 'cause he slept for most of the flight duration until he was jerked awake suddenly when the headrest, the seat and the plane began to vibrate violently, when he opened his eyes, passengers with fear—soured, drawn faces were talking dearly to one another. People with children hugged and kissed their kids, clapping them gently on their backs.

"What is happening?" he inquired from the man sitting next to him who had told him earlier that he was a retired pilot.

The plane dived and levelled, because the airflow over the wings was being disrupted by the aerodynamic stall. The vibration increased and then another dive. Some people screamed while others talked dearly to their seatmates.

"This is, I believe, a condition called 'stall condition' which is caused by flying a plane too high for its weight. This plane had been in the air for almost eight hours, it must have burnt enough fuel to reduce its weight significantly. As such the Pilot is supposed to reduce the altitude of the plane because the altitude of an airplane is dependent on its weight. The plane needs to lose altitude now but probably the pilots have not checked their travel chart to find the suitable altitude for the plane relative to its weight at the present moment. But don't worry, it will be all right. It may also be a 'stall buffet' — that's when the airflow over the plane surface and wings are breaking down and renders the wings without lift," said the man confidently, a distant curious glint in his eyes.

A pause.

"Though stalls at normal cruising speed are rare and besides the inbuilt early warning system of the plane should've informed the pilots of the oncoming stall buffet and they in return ought to have corrected the altitude of the plane before this havoc, but nevertheless don't you worry, you will see your family, friends, the beaches in Rio," added the man, patting Dave on his shoulder gently as the plane vibrated even more violently.

His explanations were soothing to Dave, but he felt afraid on remembering that if anything happened to the plane at the velocity it was going and at the altitude, that there would be no survivors; no cleverness, intelligence and strength could save him. Dave was very frightened.

"Do you live in Rio?" asked the man.

"No, I live in Paris," Dave lied.

"Do you have business there in Rio?" continued the man.

"No, I'm going on holidays to see the Carnival," replied Dave, turning to look at the man more closely.

"Looks like someone in the intelligence trade," he thought.

He avoided asking him questions to cut the conversation short. He had never got so intimate with a stranger within such a short time while on a gangster mission.

But it was because of the so-called stall buffet. It is very funny how people get close when they sense death. Though Dave enjoyed his consolations and explanation of the flight situation he would've preferred to be left in silence that prevailed most of the duration, as would most people troubled by many crimes and vices.

Chapter 18
Rio de Janeiro, Brazil

Dave drove the rest of the distance to Copacabana tumbling in thought. He drove into the car hire depot and reported the car stereo theft. He paid the difference, and was given another car. As he neared an estate office, he slowed to let a brand new Toyota Cressida driven by a lady who seemed to be in her late twenties join the traffic. He heard a hoot of impatience from behind and from the side mirror he saw two teenagers inside a fairly new black Fiat car behind him, he moved on. The teenagers drove past him and sped forward to the white Toyota. They hooted and flashed the car's headlamp at the lady to call her attention. She pulled up on the road shoulder. The guy in the front passenger seat of the Fiat came down gently and walked up to the lady, pretending to be reading or having difficulty reading a business card he was holding in his hand. As he got to the car and the lady dipped her head out the window to see what it was, the teenager dipped his hand under his shirt and brandished a short gun from under his waist belt – a .38 calibre.

Alerted, Dave slowed down. Watching the movement of his lips, Dave noticed him say in what he guessed to be a low, cold and hoarse but audible enough voice:

"Este e um assalto, fica frio. Sair de carro e nao resista por que eu mão gusta de usar este no meu vitimas. Se voce obedecer, voce saira illesa," said the boy.

"This is a robbery. Stay cool. Get out of the car. Please do not object because I hate to use this, the gun, on my victims. Just obey the orders and you won't be hurt," Dave guessed, and he was pretty right in his interpretation.

The lady got out of the car panicking, leaving everything including her handbag and her cellular phone in the car. The boy got into the car and screeched away and his colleague sped after him. Dave got out of his car and walked up to the lady who slumped onto the ground, confused and fear stricken. She didn't trust Dave at first, as he tried to speak to her and offered his hand to pull her off the ground.

"I'm a friend," said Dave, stretching a hand to her. "It's all over, they're gone," he added.

"Voce e gringo?" she asked, having noticed Dave's accent.

"Yes I am," replied Dave.

"Are you one of them?" she asked.

"No, I'm not," replied Dave, without offence, 'cause he knows how it is, it will take her some time to trust anybody in the vicinity.

"Oh, my car! Oh, if only they will send me back my handbag, I've got a lot of documents inside the bag – it's not yet five months I owned the car, a gift from my master," she complained.

"But it's alright, you are safe and unscratched, you might even get your car back, probably they need it for something, say an escape, they might drop it off somewhere for you," Dave said, trying to console her in a risible broken Portuguese.

"Eh?" she said, half hopefully and half questioning, not quite sure if she understood what he said.

"Sim," said Dave.

"Do you speak English?" Dave inquired.

"Yes I do," she replied crisply.

"Where are you going to?" Dave asked.

"To, ehmm . . ." she hemmed, trying to be evasive, then paused in thought.

"He is a gringo, harmless," she thought.

"I'm going out of Rio de Janeiro, to Angra dos Reis, some hundred and thirty kilometres south of Rio de Janeiro," she said.

"Oh, great, I'm only seeing the city. I have nothing doing. I can take you to your destination," Dave offered.

"Ehmm . . . okay," she obliged.

They drove out of Rio and had about an hour and half drive south of Rio de Janeiro before branching into a washboard road that led them to a wood gate.

A guard came out from the gate, looked into the car and smiled on recognizing Elaine, Dave's passenger.

They drove past the gate and Elaine got off the car and walked to the shed, collected a bunch of keys from the guard. She climbed back into the car and they moved forward down the rough gravel road. The air became cold and fresh as they drove further down, and there was a distant boom of something that Dave as yet wasn't sure what in the distance was producing the boom, wave, storm, or what? They stopped in the front of a house. A fairly large one-storey building nestled on double sand dunes.

"Whose place is this?" asked Dave.

"My boss," Elaine replied, not looking his direction.

"Who is your boss?"

"You know him," she said.

"No I don't."

"Didn't you say you're from Europe?" she quizzed.

"Yes, I'm from Europe, England," said Dave.

"Then you know him," affirmed Elaine.

"But who is this Brazilian that every European knows and must know?" said Dave.

"Do you like football?" asked Elaine.

"Yes I do," Dave said, his mind racing.

"It's the King's house," said Elaine.

"Whose?" asked Dave.

"The present king of soccer," replied Elaine.

"Pele?" Dave asked.

"No, the present day king," replied Elaine.

"Who is that?" asked Dave.

"The crowned Prince of football" Elaine said revealingly.

"Eh?" said Dave, not betraying the hollow feeling he experienced in the stomach out of surprise, his heart beat increasing and his body temperature few degrees higher.

"Does he live here?" asked Dave.

"No, he spends time here sometimes. It is a beach house. The beach is down there," she said, nodding in the direction of the now louder and clearer murmur of the low tide ocean waves.

"The beach is behind the house," she added. "We will go to the beach later, after cleaning the house. My boss is coming home tomorrow, he likes using the beach to tan after the winter session in Europe," she said, as she opened the front door of the house.

They went into the house and Elaine closed the front door and dropped the bunch of keys on the table in the ground floor sitting room. Dave followed Elaine from room to room as she cleaned, dusted and polished. The house has one huge master bedroom, two huge independent bedrooms, a maid's suite, a large interior sports entertainment area, a medium sized pool in the upper living room, and a satellite and video distribution system.

45 Minutes Later

"It remains the master bedroom," Elaine said to Dave as she pulled the vacuum cleaner past him and opened the door. Dave followed her into the split-level bedroom. He had a detailed glance of the room and went back into the corridor and into the living room.

As he stood by the edge of the indoor upper pool, an idea came into him and he went downstairs to the sitting room while Elaine vacuumed and polished the master bedroom. Using a pen and a piece of paper, he sketched the outline of each of the keys in the bunch on the paper.

"Gringo!" Elaine called out as he sketched the last of the keys.

"Sim!" he answered, sketched quickly, folded the paper and tucked into his pocket and ran up the wood stairs to Elaine.

CHAPTER 19

While Dave and Elaine lay supine tanning in the beach under the setting evening sun and ebb tide, the boys that snatched Elaine's car were having tyre squealing match with her car in Casa Branca, Rio de Janeiro. They won two sets and left for their hideout. They contemplated taking Elaine's car to their house or to the temporary hideout garage, aware that they had been on the city police's telescopic checklist for the last few weeks. But what worried them most was the disappearance of their friend who was sent to buy their daily dose of drugs some two weeks ago, but had not come back nor called them on the phone, and his own cell phone was switched off. They had taken a total of five stolen cars from their house garage to a friend's garage where they waited to be sold. They took the cars to their friend's a day after their friend, Balando, didn't come back from the Cocaine fetching errand.

They decided to take Elaine's car home and to bring back the other five cars in their friend's garage to their house. It had been almost two weeks, and no visit from the district police, no notice from Balando. He must've been killed and buried, probably by a rival gang. They will find this out as time goes on, or probably he is in the police net and if he had sung under pressure the house supposed to have been raided since or he didn't sing and is waiting for some time before sending them a message so that they wouldn't be implicated.

They were having a barbecue in the house, drinking beer, smoking cocktail – marijuana laced with cocaine, and snorting cocaine when their gateman rushed to the hind patio to inform them.

"One car has just sped past, then reversed at the end of the street, came towards the house and stopped some seventy meters away. I saw somebody like Balando inside the car, though I'm not sure, I didn't see his face clearly but the shirt is his and there is a man skulking around the vicinity. One of the boys went to the front upper floor balcony to look around and assess the situation. The man he saw some hours ago when he came out the balcony was still there, standing across the road, his Walkman still in place, plugged to his ears, but this time he was looking directly at him. As he turned to enter the house, the man saw a tattoo on his right shoulder. The man put his two hands above his head held them together for a second – a clue in to his colleagues up the street. Then he drew his semi-automatic pistol from the side of his black jacket and, pointing it at the guy in the balcony from across the street, crossing the street in three quick, wide steps, he shouted,

"Put your hands above your head!"

Five more men rushed to the house from a parked car down the street and they invaded the house. The guy in the hind patio of the house pulled the wall into the neighbouring compound in an effort to escape. The dogs in the neighbour's compound barked and chased after him. He ran towards the gate and into the street. He ran rightwards towards the main street of the neighbourhood.

Two policemen chased after him, and arrested him at the far end of the street and dragged him handcuffed to their car parked directly in front of their house. Inside the car was Balando, their friend.

"Sim, senhor," said Balando in response to the policeman's question.

"Him?" the policeman had asked.

They drove off to the police station with the three members of the car snatching gang aboard, all handcuffed.

Dave and Elaine stayed in the beach house until late evening. As they drove back to Rio de Janeiro, Elaine used Dave's hired mobile phone to make a call. She dialled the number of her own cellular phone and waited as it rang. It was answered at the third ring.

"Yes!" said a voice.

"Ehm, I'm the lady you robbed in the afternoon, please could I have my bag and the documents inside it," pleaded Elaine.

"I'm not a thief, I didn't rob you," said the voice.

"But . . ." Elaine insisted.

"I'm a policeman," rejoined the captain. "Come immediately to the forty-fourth district police station to identify your belongings," added the police captain.

Forty-five minutes later, Dave and Elaine were in

the police station. Elaine identified the two thieves and had her belongings and car back.

Dave silently wished the guys good luck as they sat on the bare cemented floor of the police cell, their faces swollen from hard beating and their eyes bloodshot. They reminded him of his precarious hold-up career, especially the last two that earned him his present permanent job as a Mafia hit man.

* * *

Dave was having a stroll in the neighbourhood and went past a car sales depot and noticed a guard holding a newspaper wide open before him in a read-ready position. On a casual glance one got the impression that he was reading but on a more curious and closer glance Dave noticed that the guy was asleep. He walked quietly into the depot.

"If caught," he thought, "I will say I'm coming in to obtain information on the prices of the cars."

He went behind the sleeping guard and grabbed his .45 calibre from its holster. The guard jerked awake but he was already under gunpoint, his own gun in the hands of a stranger, pointing at his temple.

"Please don't kill me, I'm a family man, my wife, my children will need me. Don't hurt me, please," the guard pleaded.

"Be quiet!" Dave hissed at him.

"Up!" he ordered.

The guard got apprehensively to his feet, his hands above his head, and Dave marched him into the administrative block of the depot, down the long corridor that holds office rooms on either side.

"Where is the washroom?" Dave asked.

"At the end of the corridor," replied the guard.

Dave led him to the end of the corridor, into the washroom.

"The phone and the radio, here," Dave ordered, stretching out his hand to the guard. He gave him his phone and walkie-talkie.

"On your ankles," shouted Dave, pointing at the handcuffs strapped on the guard's waist belt. The guard unfastened the handcuffs from his waist belt and cuffed his ankles.

"Put your hands behind you," shouted Dave. The guard obliged, and Dave handcuffed him.

"It is very tight," the guard complained.

Dave bent and tightened it two notches tighter. "Are you ok now?"

The guard didn't answer but swallowed dry.

Dave collected a good measure of tissue paper in his hand.

"Haaah," signalled Dave, opening his mouth wide. The guard opened his mouth in repetition of what Dave signalled.

Dave stuffed him with the tissue paper and taped his lips with an adhesive tape he found on the washroom windowsill. He left the guard in the washroom and went to search the offices. The drawers in the first office he went into were full of keys and key holders. In the second office room, the drawers were stuffed with sheets of papers, receipts, and car license plates heaped at one edge of the room. In the third office room, he found addressed envelopes in the drawers, twenty envelopes addressed with names and positions of functionaries in the car depot. It was the penultimate day of the month. He ripped one of the envelopes open and saw crisp notes of £50. He put the envelopes, twenty of them, into his jacket pocket. He unloaded the .45 calibre and went back into the washroom where the guard was locked up and dropped the bullets and the unloaded gun on the washroom floor.

"Alright, family man, here is your gun and good luck!" he said. "Bad to sleep on duty, huh?" he added as he closed the washroom door.

He ran down the corridor to the front of the depot and disappeared into the street. The whole operation was recorded by the closed circuit system of the depot; a clean hold-up, however, Dave never knew the depot belonged to Johnny Bandit's Brixton Mob.

The second time Dave had a run-in with the Mob's interest was when in blissful ignorance he'd pulled over a dwarf wall into a compound, the Brixton Mob's private guesthouse. He darted across the patio and pushed open the back door that stood ajar. As he stepped into the foyer entrance he heard footsteps coming towards him. He tiptoed behind the door and waited.

A guard had heard the impact of Dave's feet as he landed on the marbled floor of the compound. The guard went past the now wide open door and walked apprehensively into the vestibule, now in plain view to Dave from behind the door where he was hiding.

"Freeze!" growled Dave. "Drop your gun quietly on

the floor, kick it backwards with the heel of your boot and move four steps forward, and don't try anything smart, otherwise I blow you and the whole building up. Your family will miss you and I bet you won't like it, will you?" said Dave.

The guard froze, his mind racing, the muscle of his sole tightening inside his boot pressing against the floor, the arch of his feet curving inwards, lifting the heels slowly off the floor to spring into an acrobatic tumble and disarm the menacing voice.

"Drop your gun now, I mean now," barked Dave as the pager in his pocket began beeping. Olga, his girl-friend, was paging him. Dave's heart skipped but he was fast to turn the beeping sound into his advantage as he started a count down.

"Four! Three! Two! One . . ." he counted.

The guard in confusion had thought it was the beep-ing sound of a bomb, 'cause Dave had talked of blowing the whole place up. The guard crouched and dropped his gun, kicked it backwards with the heel of his boot and moved four steps forward as he was ordered.

Dave slunk out from behind the door and picked the gun and aiming the back of his head, avoiding his thorax as he might be wearing a bullet proof vest. He moved towards the guard and led him into the adjacent room – the kitchen.

"Lie on your stomach with both hands stretched forward beyond your head," ordered Dave. The guard obliged dutifully.

Dave walked up to the large deep freezer at the end of the fairly large kitchen and opened it. The freezer was empty, with a few blocks of ice.

"Over here!" he ordered.

The guard hurried to his feet and moved towards him, his mind whirling, contemplating a martial art style disarming. Dave saw the look in his eyes and took two steps backwards.

"In there!" he barked, pointing into the freezer.

The man looked at him pleadingly, but Dave had no time to waste on compassionate glances.

"In there, and fast!" he growled.

The guard pulled into the freezer, and Dave pushed the door close and locked it. He looked around the kitchen, his eyes followed the electric cord from the freezer to the socket. He moved forward and unplugged it. The rooms on the ground floor were empty and tidy.

Dave tiptoed up the stairs to the upper floor of the house into a room directly opposite the staircase. The room had a table and a chair to one end, a radio and a desktop personal computer on it.

He tiptoed to the door at the other side of the room, pushed it open into a large dimly lit room with a queen sized bed in the center and two naked couples sleeping peacefully, their thoraxes and abdomens inflating and deflating in a rhythmic movement as they breathed in and out, as is biologically required by nature.

Kassey Ramsey, the Mob commander had told his wife he'd be going to Liverpool on a business trip and wouldn't be coming back in two days. He had been with his American girlfriend in the guesthouse since she flew into London from New York on a Concorde airplane the previous day.

Dave looked them over for three seconds, contemplated what to do with them. – "Wake them up or leave them", he contemplated

He decided not to disturb them. He saw two wallets on the table and emptied the contents into his pocket. He picked up the gold Pateke Philip wristwatch on the table, examined it, the BMC diamond inscription on the watch glittering in the gloomy room. He pocketed it and as he opened the wardrobe, the man on the bed opened his eyes, wiped his hand across his face and squinted at Dave.

Dave signalled to him to get off the bed, guessing that he might be having a gun under the pillow.

"But who are . . .?" the man began to say.

Dave lifted his hand against his lips in a be-quiet sign, shushing him.

The man dutifully obeyed, and Dave signalled to him to put on his pyjamas and then cover the sleeping lady with the quilt. The man did as he was ordered and stood with his two hands on his head as Dave ransacked the wardrobe, pocketing money and items. When he was satisfied, he waved the man into the wardrobe.

"Your guard is inside the freezer downstairs in the kitchen. When the lady wakes up in the morning, she will liberate you and you liberate your guard. I'm very sorry for the inconvenience. Good night," Dave told him before closing the wardrobe door. He tiptoed out of the room, down the stairs and walked into the kitchen where he dropped the gun on the freezer and made his way to the patio and across it. He pulled over the dwarf wall and disappeared into the dim and deserted street. Once again the operation was well recorded in the house close circuit system.

Jennifer was awakened by the noise coming from the wardrobe. Downstairs, they let the guard out of the freezer.

The Mob had never been more humiliated: the Commander robbed, his title wristwatch stolen, locked up in the wardrobe while entertaining his girlfriend in the Mob's guesthouse.

Eric, the guard, was demoted from the security sector of the Mob and sent to work in the shop-keeping sector of the Mob's chain of department stores, and Paul the car depot guard was demoted after Dave held up the car depot. Paul was sent to work in the Mob's agricultural farm in Australia.

The Mob's intelligence noted after watching the videos that the same lone and unarmed man who held up the car depot had broken into the guesthouse. In the crime world, coincidence is not admissible, but this looked more like a coincidence than the hunting of the Mob's interests by a lone unarmed man.

"He is only good in his art," said the Mob's chief intelligence officer.

CHAPTER 20
London, England

Dave was in a pub in Kingscross, irritation creeping into him as Olga didn't appear. He glanced at the wrist-watch strapped on his left wrist and frowned. Olga was twenty-five minutes late. She'd said it was an hour session before crossing the street into the hotel to attend to her last client of the night.

The waiter placed the beer glass on the table, his eyes fixed on the watch on Dave's wrist.

"What a nice watch you've got, what make is it?" he asked.

"Pateke Philippe," Dave replied.

Back at the counter, the waiter told the bar man of Dave's watch.

Dave gulped down the last of the beer in the glass

and signalled for a refill. The bar man came hurrying with a glass of beer on a tray.

Dave's left hand was resting on the table.

"Is it ten o'clock yet, sir?" he asked, stretching to see what time it was on the watch. The BMC diamond inscription was glittering and unmistakable.

"Not yet, it's five minutes to ten," replied Dave, without looking at his face.

"Enjoy your drink," said the bar man and walked back to the counter. At the counter, he put a call through to the Mob's Lieutenant Commander – Comrade Harvey. In fifteen minutes, three men walked into the pub and after speaking with the bar man, they walked to Dave's table and one after the other they unbuttoned their blazers, flapping them open enough to show Dave the pistols tucked into their waist belts, without the guys sitting at the next table seeing it.

Dave was frightened.

"Please, gentleman, accompany us out of the pub," one of them ordered.

Dave obliged without the least of objections. They marched out of the pub without raising an eyebrow. They got into a waiting car outside and drove off.

Dave wasn't sure why he's being driven away and to where, but he was sure that the men weren't policemen or state security men of any sort. He was being kidnapped. He thought of Olga; what had become of her and why had she kept him standing? If any thing happened to him, she would be very lonely and vulnerable. He loved Olga immensely. He closed his eyes and offered a silent prayer that God protect her.

The car was now speeding along the highway, heading to Brixton.

"What's happening and where are you taking me to?" Dave asked.

The man sitting to his right shushed him down. "Ssshhh!" he shushed.

The other man by his left lifted his hand and glanced at the wristwatch, the BMC diamond inscription glittered in the rather dim car interior.

"Brixton Mob Commander," he murmured to himself. They had been travelling for twenty-five minutes now. They turned off right into an uncluttered street and three minutes down the street they went left then straight down until they stopped at the traffic light. They waited for the light to turn, drove past the lamp posts and turned right into a quiet street with detached houses. Past five houses, they drove into a gated beige-painted house and into the garage. Dave was led through a door inside the garage into a sitting room.

"Sit down," one of the men said.

Dave selected a one-seater cushion and slumped into it. The guy who was sitting to his left in the car came over to him, bent down and lifted his left hand and unfastened the watch off Dave's wrist and put it in a saucer and walked away. Dave watched him climb the stairs, taking the steps two at a time.

Upstairs, Comrade Harvey collected the watch form the saucer, examined it closely and nodded in approval.

"Put him in the cellar till tomorrow morning," he ordered.

A door opened somewhere behind Dave and two men came into the living room, moving towards him from behind. They grabbed him, each holding him on one arm and they dragged him across the room into a dark corridor and stopped at a door. One of them flickered a switch on, opened the door, and they went down a short staircase into the cellar. At the opposite end of the cellar was a black metal coffin and two candles, one standing at either end.

One of the men moved forward and picked up a gun-shaped lighter and lit the candles and opened the coffin. Dave noticed tiny circular openings arranged into a circle at the tail end of the coffin's lid and similar holes arranged into a cross at the head of the coffin's lid.

"In there!" one of the men told him, nodding towards the coffin.

Dave trudged forward like a man to the scaffold and stepped into the coffin and lay supine, closing his eyes. He went blank in the head when the man banged the coffin lid, closing and barring it.

In the morning, after a night that seemed to Dave an eternity, he heard the clicking sound of the door as it opened and footsteps marched into the cellar and to the coffin.

"The long awaited time has come, not for the men, but for my end," he thought.

All along he'd been afraid and pessimistic. As the men unbarred the coffin and opened it, Dave offered what he believed was his last prayer. Even in his confusion and weakness he reaffirmed to himself and God that he had accepted Jesus Christ as his Lord and Saviour. He asked for forgiveness for all his trespasses and reminded God that though he accepted the Word right inside the coffin, he, almighty God, had said that no time is too late.

"And God, my Lord, remember what you said through Jesus Christ in John Chapter 5 verses twenty-four to twenty-six. Amen," he prayed as the coffin flipped open and a man offered him a hand. As Dave gripped it, he pulled him up to his feet and Dave stepped out of the coffin and staggered from dizziness, his muscles and veins stiff and sore. They led him out of the cellar into the corridor and to a patio behind the house and into a cottage where he had his bath in a white tiled bathroom. He brushed his teeth using the toothbrush they offered him. He was served tea, toasted bread, bacon, and an omelette for his breakfast in a kitchen with small dining table and two dining chairs.

After the breakfast, he was offered a new and well-ironed pair of pants, a shirt and shoes. As he sat waiting and thinking what would be his fate, one of the men came forward to him.

"You held up the car depot and the guest house. True

or false?" he asked.

"True," replied Dave. "But, I . . ." continued Dave.

"No apologies to me, wrong quarter for apologies," interrupted the man.

"Let's go," he said to Dave, signalling to him to get to his feet and follow him.

The two men led Dave into the sitting room in the outer main house where Comrade Harvey, flanked by two Mob intelligence officers, was waiting.

Dave was ushered to a seat opposite the three men, the same seat he'd chosen last night. The two men bowed their greetings to Comrade Harvey.

"True," one of them said out loud.

Comrade Harvey looked sideways at the men flanking him with a knowing glance, nodded, and dismissed the two men that brought Dave into the room with a wave of the hand.

"I'm Comrade Harvey and this is Senior Clayton and Senior Foster," said Harvey, looking at each of the men in turn as he introduced them.

"I'm Dave Scotts," Dave said timidly.

"Do you work for any group or with any person?" asked Harvey.

"No, I work alone," said Dave, looking at the floor, his head bowed.

"Look up straight into our faces when you answer," Clayton said to him.

"Yes, sir," Dave answered, looking up.

"You are good at hold-ups, eh?"

"Yeah," replied Dave, not knowing if he was answering correctly.

"You like crime, don't you?"

"Yes I do," replied Dave.

"You know how it is in the crime world, don't you?"

"I do, sir," Dave replied.

"From today on, you stay with us, you do hold up jobs and go on general errands when need be, understand?"

"Yes sir," said Dave.

"The humourists will explain to you how it works here," said Comrade Harvey and got to his feet. The two intelligence officers followed him and they took the steps to the upper floor of the house.

They had barely disappeared into the upper floor when the two men that had brought Dave into the sitting room marched back into the room and dragged him away, holding him by either arm. Dave didn't understand why they had suddenly become unfriendly again. They dragged him into the cellar where three other men were waiting. The cellar have been rearranged, a table covered with white cloth was now at the center. Two of the three men approached Dave while one started unfastening his waist belt, undid his zip and pulled his pants down to his ankle. The other undid his shirt buttons. The two men holding him on either arm lifted him off the floor, so that the one crouching before him pulled off his shoes and pants. Dave wriggled in protest but he was weak and the two men on his either side were a lot stronger. Besides, Dave knew he couldn't win against five armed and determined men. In half a minute Dave was stripped stark naked. He was strapped to a chair and his hair shorn off. Dave watched one of the guys curled his fingers into a fist and struck him hard on the right eye. Dave felt stars diverging from his eyes. The man hit him again on the top right of his head, the blow heavier this time. Another blow descended on the top left of his head then a foot chop landed on his neck. The big man who'd been sitting quietly by the corner watching every detail of the happenings, smoking a cigarette, came forward to Dave and stubbed out the cigarette butt on Dave's scalp. Dave growled, moaned, and then spat at the man. The man looked at him scornfully, turned and went back to his corner.

"Quieten him and put him in the cooler," he ordered.

Dave was gagged, unfastened from the chair and put inside the freezer beside the coffin where he had slept the previous night. He was brought out from the freezer after fifteen minutes and laid on his stomach on the table and strapped tightly in place. He felt the coldness of the copper wire as the men ringed it around his ankle and his left wrist.

"On!" he heard the big man's voice as the electric current engrossed on him and took its toll of torture on him.

The voice went again.

"Off!"

"On!"

"Off!"

"On!", for the next fifteen minutes.

And one after the other, the other four men stubbed out their cigarette butts on his scalp. Dave moaned until he was left with no energy to moan and took the pains in quietude.

Someone grabbed his scrotum, press his ball with a plastic plier, he pressed it hard, released and hard again. The pain was killing and Dave moaned and fainted. The men nursed him back to consciousness. When he opened his eyes the big man came around the table and bent forward until his face was inches from Dave's.

"It remains one more session and you will be free, and free forever," said the big man.

The man with a jackknife size electric saw started from the tip of Dave's left toe and sawed it down, splitting his toe down to the ball of the foot, blood gushed out staining the white sheet on the table. He poured a purple solution of iodine on the wound before putting the ligature tightly on the toe. Dave wriggled and wriggled in pain, his eyes rolling wildly but to no avail, he couldn't help but take the hit and cried himself to sleep. He woke up in the evening on a bed in the cottage. At the edge of the bed was a bunch of flowers with a card. He opened the card and read the single sentence, "The Mob loves you Dave".

Among the flowers was an unloaded Russian-made

.45 automatic pistol. As Dave examined the gun, the door opened and the big man entered into the room. Dave's heart skipped. The man saw the fear in his eyes.

"Don't be afraid, Dave, the humour session is over. My name is Walter," he said, taking his seat on the single chair in the room. The four other guys that participated in the torture session entered the room one after the other.

"We are the Mob's humourists," Walter began when all had entered the room. "What you underwent is called humour in the Mob, or at least it is Johnny's brand of humour. In the actual sense it is meant to teach one that in crime, like the Commander says: 'You've got to be mean, tough, hardened, deliberate, no sentiments, no remorse.' Because whenever something goes wrong, that will be the kind of treatment you may receive from your captors. It is not a punishment or torture as you might see it, but the initiation into the Mob so that when you go on an errand and something goes wrong, the Mob will be rest assured that you won't squeal on the Mob under the most heinous torture because we'd be sure that there is nothing they can do to you that Johnny Bandit's humorists haven't done to you.

"Dave," he called out, stepping forward to the edge of the bed, stretching out his hand to Dave. Dave sat up on the bed and took the heavy hand in a firm grip.

"Johnny Bandit and the Mob welcomes you to banditry," said Walter, looking Dave straight in the eye.

The four men took his hand in turn and welcomed him to banditry.

It was the start of a hit man career in the Mafia world – the London Brixton Mafia clan.

It took two months for Dave to recover fully from the pains, sores and the wound on his toe, and since then he's been on the Johnny Bandit's Brixton Mob payroll, on a £5,000 monthly salary and a retirement and pension plan. And today here is Dave, thousands of miles across the globe in the forty-fourth district police station in the heart of a ghetto in Rio de Janeiro, Brazil, representing the Mob's business interest.

Chapter 21
Rio de Janeiro, Brazil

"The police are your friends," the district police chief told Elaine as he handed her the car key and her hand-bag. Dave and Elaine walked across the door into the police car park.

"Will I see you tomorrow?" Dave asked.

"Tomorrow? No, my boss will be coming home to-morrow. Next tomorrow, you can see me next tomor-row," said Elaine.

Elaine drove home in her car while Dave followed her nose to tail in escort.

It was 10:00 p.m. when Dave turned into Avenida Atlantico on his way back to his hotel. His cell phone chirped in its piercing melody.

"Dave?" came the voice when he answered the call.

"Yes, Dave," he replied.

"Your guest will be home tomorrow morning," the voice began without preamble. "The Boeing 737 Varig flight number 111 has just left the Heathrow airport. It will arrive in your city at 6:30 a.m. tomorrow morning. Good luck," he said, and the line went dead.

"Good luck," Dave repeated.

He'd rather not be reminded of luck when he is on a mission. He's often believed that success of his mission depends on his skill rather than lousy luck. Being reminded of luck makes him nervous but luck if needed in this mission has been met in the person of Elaine whom he knows will always and innocently keep him abreast of the daily agenda of "best" – his guest.

He had a sound, dreamless sleep that night and woke up quite early the next morning to go to the locksmith.

He counts on Ian the beachcomber to find a good locksmith to turn the outlines of the keys on the piece of paper into a tangible mould. He'd met Ian on his first night in Rio de Janeiro, and Ian had bought him the first roll of marijuana he smoked on the Copacabana beach. He thought of what Ian will think about it. He recollected the curious look in Ian's eyes as he rolled a stick of cigarette back and forth between his thumb and fore-finger to remove the tobacco inside the cigarette paper and feed the marijuana into the hollow paper and made use of the cigarette filter that will offer some protections against some noxious substances that help among others in causing emphysema – a kind of lung cancer symptomized by difficult breathing in heavy smokers.

"Why?" Ian had asked. "Why remove the tobacco?" Ian added.

Dave explained.

Ian took a test drag from the joint, shook his head sideways in disbelief, smiling vacuously.

"Este gringos inventa cada coisa. The stuff has lost its flavour," he said.

Dave stopped the car on the side park and was winding up the passenger side glass when he saw Ian running towards him across the beach sands. Ian led Dave to a locksmith in the morro de Copacabana without questions and went back to the beach with the $20 bill Dave tipped him. He'd not been bordered to wait for him to finish and Dave was glad he left.

Dave left the locksmith's place with a key ring. He tucked the bunch of keys into the car's pigeonhole and tore up the sketch and drove towards Barra de Tijuca. He joined a group of fans camping in front of "best's" mansion in the hope of catching a glimpse of the football mega star.

As dusk fell, the crowd of fans and Well Wishers began to disperse slowly. It was 7:30 p.m. when the football idol finally drove past the main gate of the mansion into the treed and quiet street. The few fans around screamed and threw airborne kisses at him. The car slowed momentarily as it approached them and the "best" waved enthusiastically to them and moved on.

Dave entered his car parked on the paved street shoulder, and sped after him. Dave closed up to a tailing distance, as "best" turned off the Tijuca Boulevard into the road leading to Rochinha.

"Rochinha? Why Rochinha?" Dave mused.

He tailed him up the morro de Rochinha past clustered streets of the ghetto to a relatively less busy and rather dusky neighbourhood. He pulled up in front of an unlit, unoccupied and unpainted house illuminated by rays of light from the adjacent and opposite houses. Dave parked his car two blocks away and waited. "Best" opened the front door of the house and entered. Dave noticed a light shine inside the house. He wondered what place it could be — a drug joint? Of course not, he undergoes anti-dope tests regularly, he doesn't use drugs. A shrine? The old home where he was born and raised?

Most probably.

Dave wondered what the inside of the house might look like — unplastered bedroom walls, uncarpeted floors, old stained plastic plates and spoons, a rickety kerosene stove in the kitchen without a dresser, all unequable to his present mega status. Dave noted with a twinge of conscience how different he is from "best". "Best" has shaken off a suffocating poverty whereas he, Dave, has come from a below average English family. A family that would be well above average were they in this part of the world, Brazil, South America. "Best" got out from the house into the open back yard, walked round the house to the frontage using the side path that separates the house from the adjacent building. He walked up the front of the adjacent house and knocked at the door. It opened at the second knock and a woman in her fifties came out, smiled broadly and embraced him warmly. They got into the house, "best" was seeing his old neighbourhood, climbing in and out his past and it seems to be his sure source of joy. The past seems to remind him of his roots, the past restrictions, fear and poverty and the present, the alpine height he'd attained that ushered in an ocean of freedom, fame and courage. In all, it helps him to dampen the burden of his fame, his success. The fame, the success, that Dave, has come to snub out, to destroy those dribble laden and elusive legs of his.

Dave wondered what would become of him after he blew off his kneecap and his career terminated. He hopes and prays that some new wave in the sports world, the very type that swept him to his present status, will see him through.

"Thank God. It isn't to kill him, it's just to stop him," Dave thought.

Dave knew he must do it and perfectly, otherwise he loses his own career and even his life, he, "best" will still have his life and time to enjoy the wealth he's amassed.

Dave looked up and down the street. The neighbourhood was quiet and dirty. Few people trickled up and down the street and a samba chorus wafted from a distant samba bar. Dave waited.

It was twenty minutes when "best" came out of the house and walked across the street to his car. Dave followed him to a nearby neighbourhood cemetery. Dave guessed he would go home the same way they came, so he turned his car to face the direction they came. Dave walked up and went into the cemetery as the dim moon high above peeped slowly out from behind the clouds. A car passed by and its headlamp illuminated the surrounding. Dave docked, he saw "best" kneeling beside a tomb, his hands held together in a praying pose.

"It must be his mother's tomb."

What an optimum place to do the hit," Dave thought, but he had no weapon on him, no gun, no jackknife. "What a missed opportunity!" hissed Dave.

"Best" was incanting now.

"Mamae, mamae, eu estou aqui. Ven falar comigo mae, vem jah. Uhoshokveil, lcabata, nouko," he invoked.

"A spiritualist?" Dave murmured to himself. He'd heard so much about spirits and ghouls. Dave saw a descending light of blinding brightness at the far end of the cemetery. The shine was gone into a ball of darkness before he could blink to see it clearly.

"Best" incanted and invoked louder and with more vehemence. The light flashed again, now right above the tomb beside which "best" was kneeling. An extraordinary quietness descended onto the graveyard, the tomb and its surroundings were covered by a thick white cloud and Dave couldn't make out the outline of "best" beside the tomb. And a white large vulture-like bird hovered around the tomb. A shower of goose pimples descended on Dave. He became numb, sleepy and then tranced. He could only hear muffled reverberating voices. The light flashed again and went dead and Dave felt the numbness drifting off him as the reverberating muffled voices subsided and "best's" throbbing voice became audible.

"Adeus mae, adeus, ate logo."

The light flashed again at the end of the cemetery where it first appeared but this time it was ascending into the quiet dimly moonlit sky.

"Best" sprang to his feet feeling revived and threaded his way out of the cemetery across the road into his car. He drove past Dave's car parked down the road but didn't take any particular notice of it. Dave hurried back to his car and drove after him. Dave had never believed in spirits, but today, he saw a mysterious blinding light and heard muffled echoing voices, the numb feeling, all must have been the besieging force from a manifest spirit.

"And what of "best"? Did he see much more than I? Did he feel the numbness?" he thought. "The muffled reverberating voice must have been the voice of the spirit giving its messages and probably "best" was able to decipher the voice and obtain his information and asked for . . . probably blessings and protection."

Did the spirit tell "best" about him, Dave? That he, Dave is lurking behind him to hamstring him and make him a spent force in the world of sports."

The hooting blasts from the line of vehicles behind brought Dave back to land. The cars in front of him had moved forward, the traffic light was green. He engaged the gear and moved forward, fear vibrating through him.

"Am I being hypnotized? Is it the spirit thing?" thought Dave as he stretched to peer forward in search of "best's" car. It was four cars ahead.

"You must always be a professional. Now you are here

in South America, you must deliver the Mob's wish. Don't get afraid of him, he's got no magical or spiritual powers and even if he's got, you've got to do what you've been sent here to do. Do it and receive the Mob's kudos or fuck it and have your own spirit be invoked and received by your next of kin," one mind reminded Dave.

Dave trailed him out of Rochinha as he kerb crawled the streets of Rio until he pulled up opposite a strip tease club. The multi-colour lights of the club were blinking atop the building and the entrance door of the club. Dave parked his car behind "best's" car, leaving a space enough to enter yet another car. "Best" was resting against his car, talking into the phone. Dave hesitated, he heard what "best" was saying and replying to someone somewhere in the town or overseas on the other end of the wireless connection, but Dave with his little understanding of the sonorous Brazilian version of the Portuguese language was able to grasp only the sketchy tenor of what was being discussed – joining the dots of his replies, Dave adduced that "best" was being invited to somewhere but he declined, saying: "I'm sorry but I will be tanning for the next two days."

Dave waited for another ten minutes after "best"

crossed the street and walked into the club before going into the club himself.

Inside the club, "best" was so happy and relaxed, the only time Dave has seen him with as happy an expression as now was in a football match, especially after scoring a goal. He discussed with friends, acquaintances, well wishers, and naked girls in G-strings and bra cups barely covering their nipples exhibiting their feminine wiles. Those he couldn't reach waved airborne kisses enthusiastically to him while others flashed a thumbs-up sign.

"The people's man," thought Dave.

Dave took a table at the end of the club in his own quiet bluff, and struggled with an inner challenging desire not to be intimidated by the glamour of "best's" stardom, knowing that his delivery or failure will result in the Mob's credit or discredit. He watched as a waiter approached "best" and listened while scribbling something on a pad and left afterwards. Minutes later, a barrage of wine corks began in all corners of the 40m by 50m split-level strip tease club.

"Compliments of the football crack, the crowned Prince of football!" the waiter shouted at each cork missile release. The naked girls in G-strings, some of whom would change into pant and skirt suits accessorized with broaches, strings and pearls the next morning on their way to their respective offices, teetered about on high heel shoes showing off their well honed butts, bosoms, and their raffish elegance.

A waiter came to Dave's table with a bucket of ice and a chilled bottle of champagne covered with a white cloth.

"Good champagne," said Dave as the waiter lifted the bottle, showing him the label.

The waiter seemed not to understand what Dave said, for he released the champagne cork and half filled the wine glass and dropped it noisily on the table.

"You ain't paying, the crack is paying for you. It is gratis," said the waiter and left.

Dave looked up at him suspiciously and kept quite. He reached the wine glass and took a sip of the champagne, not minding having his own bottle of free champagne together with a put-down.

As the night aged, and "best" consumed alcohol, his face drooped in drunkenness. Dave, though unarmed, admitted that it was a good and ample opportunity to hit him as he drove home, alone and tipsy.

The man sharing the table with Dave who had introduced himself as Ayrton beckoned to a bosomy lady to join him at the table. The girl came over to their table.

"Come home with me tonight and grace my bed," Ayrton said to the girl.

"Home, no, but for two hours in the five-star hotel some five minute drive down the street, yes," replied the lady.

"Why? I will pay you well, $1,000," said Ayrton.

"It's a generous price, but it's not for the money. I will be going home about a little after midnight. That's the reason, you see, I've not taken any alcoholic drink today, because I will study tonight. I have a court hearing at 4:00 p.m. tomorrow," said the lady.

"What did you commit?" asked Ayrton.

"No, I'm a defence lawyer," replied the lady.

"You?" asked Ayrton.

"Yes, me, I'm a lawyer," said the lady, rolling her eyes seductively.

"You mean . . . then why are you here?" asked Ayrton.

"I'm here to have fun, to have my own share of dick.

Look, I started coming here some six months ago, since my life I've been, yes I can say, sex starved. In the secondary school I graduated a virgin. In the law school I lost my virginity to my first boyfriend, a courtship that lasted for two years. Since then, it has been very difficult to find a man. I used an electric vibrator I named Dave for the six years that I stayed in Miami. I got so addicted to it that at a time I cared much less about men and the real blood throbbing, vein-wired penis. When I came to discover how much I was dependent on Dave, my electric vibrator . . ."

At the mention, Dave became animated, then relaxed upon realizing it was only a coincidence.

"It seemed as if I've forgotten how to win a man, how to culture a man that I like into a courtship. It's like I've forgotten how to live normally sexually. Every morning before going to work, I will visit Dave, when I'm on recess in the office I will visit Dave. If I see a man on the street and I like him I will visit Dave when I get home, with the man's image in my memory. Instead of walking up to him and chatting him up or work out a plan to win him over and with luck bring him home to my bed someday. At a time I felt that America and its on-your-own way of life was the problem so I left America and came here back to Brazil to catch a man, my own Dave, a natural one.

"Once in Brazil, I decided never to visit Dave and I stayed six months but to no avail. I couldn't find a man, I felt my vaginal hole rusting, it was a six months without anything live or artificial wriggling inside me, moving in and out of me, filling my womanly hole, then withdrawing and moving in again, without nothing clicking my clitoris making me to moan out loud in pleasure – mesmerizing me. After being tempted by three lesbians, I went back to Dave. Poor thing, he was starved too. Then after three months, on one rainy evening, looking out my window, watching the low grey heavy clouds scudding across the threatening sky and dropping light showers of rain as they scudded forward, I assured myself that, there are many heterosexual men out there, that God decorated the world with lots of natural Daves, of many sizes, colours and texture and I was stuck with a dumb, deaf Dave – a man-made dick that never talked to me, never kissed me, hugged me nor looked into my eyes, right into my pupils to tell me how wonderful, how delicious and how much I knew to make him crazy on the bed, even if it was all lies, sweet nothings that make one feel human, feel like a real woman, you know, to baby that child in me. Then I decided that I must reach out for a real Dave, a natural penis. That I must get it as a normal working class professional or as a call girl, whichever way but a real blood-throbbing veined dick inside me, mesmerizing my sexual being. It's been six months I started coming here and I had never been happier. The business here is very exciting, the fun, the detachment of each partner, each party just concerned with the pleasure he is deriving. The man trying his maximum to derive a pleasure commensurate to the money he will dish out at the end, and in so doing, hits it where it thrills and rivets the most sending me to the high heavens, to paradise as my womanly secretions lubricates the track elevating his desire, his lust. At the end of a session, some men had mixed feelings if I refused to accept payment from them. In my opinion, they often think I was scheming for something, something more than the money, but they were wrong because I've got what I sought in them, the natural Dave. I only take money from men who couldn't mesmerize me with their dicks, yes those ones pay. They deserve to pay.

"So like I said earlier, I'm not here for money, I'm here to have my own share of sexual pleasure, to source for sexual fun. But if you choose to believe that I'm a whore, well that's what it seems but it takes two to tango. And if tangoing with you is what it means to be a whore, then I say, let it be," she said, stretching out her hand to him. He took it and she pulled him up to his feet.

Dave watched them walk towards the ladies dressing room and minutes later he saw them cross the entrance doorway and disappeared from sight into the outer streets. Dave, an all time friend to a call girl, understood the lady very well.

He thought of Olga. Is she alive or dead? What is she doing now, staying with a client, thinking of him, Dave? Does she . . .

Dave saw "best" walk past the entrance doorway, flanked by two men. He got to his feet and made for the exit. As he tailed them to Barra de Tijuca, he admitted to himself that even if he had his weapons there would always be a mob of friends, hangers-on to hinder any hit attempt, but nevertheless it was a good night for Dave, it gave him enough of "best's" off the record profile.

The reception hall was quiet and deserted when Dave arrived at the hotel. The receptionist heard his footsteps and came out from the inner office as he walked up to the reception counter. He handed Dave his room key and a folded piece of paper.

Dave unfolded the paper immediately and read, "Elaine called twice, will call again much later," read the message.

"Thanks!" he said to the receptionist and walked to the elevator.

"Boa noite senhor," replied the receptionist.

The telephone peeped with a call as Dave stepped into his room. Dave reached for the phone. Elaine was on the line. She'd just come back from Angra dos Reis, where she'd gone to drop some edibles and other necessities in the beach house. Her boss would be going down there tomorrow evening with a cook to tan for two days. She might be going together with them but she wasn't sure yet, it will all depend on the boss and how many assistants he will need hanging around and ministering to him while he tans. If she happened not to go with them, she would call Dave and come over to his hotel to spend the Sunday evening with him.

"Boa noite," Elaine crooned.

"Good night," Dave replied.

Dave didn't like the timing of the call. Is somebody monitoring him as he tails the "best"? He is an innocent tourist as far as the eyes can see. It's just coincidence that Elaine called as he came in.

As he lay on the bed courting sleep, he ruminated on the odd prospect of Elaine going down to the beach house with her boss. He's often hated killing women and children, because if Elaine would be there in the beach house, he would have to kill her, no other choice, to prevent any comebacks.

Chapter 22
London, England

It was 9:00 a.m. Brazilian time and 1:00 p.m. Prime Meridian time when Dave left the hotel for the cruise line office. Jane was sitting comfortably in the owner's side at the back of the black Mercedes Benz saloon car, her bodyguard sat in the front passenger seat, a .38 calibre planted accessibly on his thighs as the driver, his white baseball cap tipped over his forehead, speeded along the MI4 highway to get home on or before 2:00 p.m. when the "highest" wakes from his Sunday afternoon siesta.

Two ambulances, one bore the markings of a British charity, the other the markings of the British nuclear fuel and a sign, "Danger, radioactive" on its plate number, overtook the black Mercedes car, and were followed by a Honda car that seemed to be using the opportunity to move forward while the two ambulances raced forward, sirens wailing, the Honda car careened before the Mercedes Benz car and then a brown Labrador dog jumped down its rear window and scampered around frantically as tyres screeched and cars swerved to avoid hitting the dog. Fifty metres ahead, the two ambulances halted diagonally to the road, blocking the road, thick white plume of smoke fumes spewed from the ambulance with the nuclear fuel markings and three masked men jumped down the vehicle, one bent onto the front tyres while the other opened the vehicle bonnet and got busy finding and correcting a non-existent fault in the engine. A third man stood at the middle of the road with a medium sized red flag, "BNFL – Radioactive" boldly printed in red ink on it, held up high above his head in a "Halt – Danger" sign.

The occupants of the cars beyond rolled up their glasses, afraid that the ambulance might be ferrying a dangerous radioactive.

Except for their names and faces at a very close look, the whole set-up is a perfect replica of the black Mercedes Benz car and its occupant stacked up on the MI4 highway. The lady sitting at the owner's back seat of the car was wearing a brown body hugging mini dress, the same merely brushed-back, shoulder length, and legally blonde hair and no makeup as Jane —"highest's" wife. The man on the front passenger seat had a black leather jacket on, a .45 calibre gun on his thigh. The driver had his white baseball cap tipped over his forehead, as the shiny black Mercedes Benz car with the same plate number as Jane's approached the mansion gate at normal speed. The driver smiled – the usual mere show of the teeth as the gatekeeper looked their direction and the gate rolled slowly open. They drove into the compound and followed the private driveway signs to the garage, the garage doors rolled open when the car was at a ten meter distance from it and rolled back to close as the car got into the garage. The guy in the front seat sprang out, walked round the car to the trunk and collected the first aid box and made for the elevator, and pressed the button, signalling up. The elevator ascended and stopped at the upper floor of the building. He stepped out of the elevator car into a twenty square foot sky blue granite floored foyer that overlooked a large bedroom beyond. He was humbled by the rich architectural grandeur of the environment, tastefully decorated, a flowing inside-to-out transparent glass wall that gave a stunning panoramic view of the compound. The multi-level garden courtyard with a reflecting exterior pool and a nine meters waterfall all adds to the grandeur. The soothing somnolent sound from the large Jacuzzi between the room and the foyer, rhyming with the deep and even breathing of the world's highest-paid footballer lying peacefully, vulnerable and undefended on the three metre radius circular bed covered to his neck with a sparkling white quilt, graced the rather cool atmosphere. He stood stunned over the Jacuzzi, observing the gracefulness of the fabulous environment with a consummate relish. His silencer fitted .45 calibre shot gun aiming the temple of the slumbering man, and his index finger well positioned to trigger a shoot at the slightest suspicious movement. He moved quietly towards the bed and standing at the edge, he pulled the quilt to cover the sleeping man's face and head, exposing his body. He pushed the nose of the gun to the left side of his chest pressing it hard against his flesh so that he felt the coldness of the metal.

"Highest" wriggled and tried to shout but the quilt

covering his face muffled his shouting.

"Be quiet," said the menacing voice of the man.

On hearing the cold harsh voice, and feeling the coldness of a metal on his chest, "highest" kept calm and pleaded that he be left to live. The man cuffed his ankles and his wrists.

"Close your eyes," he ordered.

"Highest" closed his eyes as ordered and pleaded once again for his life.

"Please don't hurt me, take whatever but let me live," he pleaded, his voice throbbing with fear.

The man opened the first aid box and brought out a meter long black strip of cloth and blindfolded him. He reached the medical box again for the scalpel, cotton wool, adhesive tape and a roll of bandage. He unpicked a short length of the adhesive tape and gagged "highest". He rolled him to his stomach and reached for the syringe filled with anaesthesia and pulled off the hypodermic needle protector, and pushed the needle into the vein in the ankle region and slowly pushed down the plunger. Using the scalpel, he visited the sinew behind his both ankles. He wrapped the chunk in a piece of cloth and placed it inside a small plastic packet and into the first aid box. He looked at his wrist watch, he had only three minutes left, the operation was supposed to last only twenty minutes. He placed a good measure of cotton wool over each cut on each of the ankles and bandaged it to place, to stop the profuse bleeding. He packed the first aid box, closed it and lit for the elevator and into the waiting car in the garage. They drove out of the garage and headed for the gate.

The man crouching over the ambulance engine on the M14 highway glanced at his wristwatch. It had been twenty minutes that he'd been working on the engine. He closed the bonnet, went into the car and pressed deep on the fume-release pedal, releasing more thick white fumes of oxygen into the air. On noticing more fumes, the man holding up the "Halt – Danger" flag, folded his flag and went into the ambulance. The third man went behind the driving wheel and they screeched away. The Honda car driver struggled with the ignition of his car, apparently having problems firing the engine. The tailgate of the articulated lorry was lowered onto the highway at a thirty degrees slope some two hundred metres down the highway. The two ambulances ran up the tailgate slope into the trailer. The lorry driver pressed a button and the tailgate lifted slowly up into place and the lorry charged down the highway, mission accomplished. The London traffic cops ran down the entire length of the highway but never found the broken-down ambulance that caused the traffic jam that would take the next fifteen hours to correct.

The gatekeeper of "highest's" mansion pressed the red stop button of his cellular phone, a flame of anger, hate and jealousy kindling in him. The husky voice he heard in the background as he conversed with his wife was unmistakably Daniel's. He was inquiring from his wife if it's him, Luke, on the line. The wife didn't answer him verbally but must've nodded her yes. His neighbour had once told him that Daniel spends his days in his house while he's at work but he didn't suspect anything because during the time of the report, Daniel was doing a plumbing repair in his house and he's been a very good friend of the family, highly above suspicion. But now, today at this time, Daniel has no reason to be in his house alone with his wife and most suspiciously his wife didn't tell him that Daniel was in there in the house with her. That alone would've decoursed any sprouting suspicion. And again her voice, the sexual huskiness in the voice, she'd always sounded like that when he called her, but he'd thought it was for him, that just hearing his voice over the phone when he's not at home inflamed her desire for him just like any wife in love with her husband but now he knows it's always been for Daniel. He could imagine his wife taking her bath, creaming her skin and finally wriggling into her most fitting dress and a high heel shoe to model for Daniel to make him want her and approve of her and then running into Daniel's open arms, embraced and held crushingly against his chest, his tongue finding hers and kissing her sloshily, her clitoris stiff and her vagina wet and Daniel's dick straining for a stroke. Daniel running his finger down her back to her butt, cupping her butt tightly in his palms then lifting her dress and pulling it off, pushing her onto the bed – his matrimonial bed then with his one hand unzipped his pants exposing his dick and his wife guiding him into her, and Daniel thrusting back and forth inside her. A sense of isolation and betrayal besieged him and a dangerous rage coursing through him. He looked up at the approaching car and into the distance, ruminating on the best punishment for the Judases. He slowly and numbly reached and pressed the gate button at the third hoot from the black Mercedes. The gateman's delay at opening the gate already betokened danger to the occupants of the black Mercedes and they all got ready for action. It is the contingency plan to shoot their way home in case of any obstacle. They mustn't get caught in the star's home, otherwise they would be lynched. Cutting and hamstringing the star is like hamstringing the people's happiness, their source of joy and the excitement.

A refreshing smile lit up their tension-frozen faces as the car rolled through the gateway to a disappearing mission.

Chapter 23
Angra dos Reis
Rio de Janeiro, Brazil

Dave was speeding on the high sea towards Angra do Reis, he'd hired a motorboat equipped with an inflatable kayak and a battery operated hand air pump. It was a clear breezy day and the sea was desolate, the damp sea wind ruffling his blond hair as the boat knotted its way across the sea, sending ripples across the surface of the ocean. The white sandy beach came to view and Dave slowed and steered the boat towards the heavy foliage shore out of view from the beach house. The tide was not yet at its peak and the surf broke with slight claps. Dave looked around for a place to beach the boat. Under the rolling waves he saw a shark marauding in the water. It was the shark season in Brazil, sharks that are attracted to the city's beaches by warm ocean currents that attract fishes close to the shore. Dave steered the boat to a stop and inflated the kayak with the hand pump. He put the first aid medical bag and the narrow roll of rug carpet into the kayak and paddled away from the foliage shore towards the private beach — "best's" private beach.

As he paddled forward, a shark charged towards him. Dave saw the shark quite on time but had little to do other than paddle more rapidly forward to get to the beach quickly. The shark attacked the scull and Dave struck the scull into the water to hit the shark but the scull slapped on the water and swerved, missing the shark. The shark bit and held fast on the scull with its strong pointed shiny fangs and pulled. Dave was caught unawares by the force of the pull. It was a split second decision; if he held onto the scull the shark would pull him right into the water and move in for the kill, so he released the scull and held onto the sides of the kayak but the force of the pull was already exerting its toll. The kayak overturned, sending Dave head-on into the water but he held fast and strong onto the sides of the kayak. In his upturned position he saw the shark charge towards him, he tried to shout but his mouth was filled with water, muffling the shout and it died in his throat. He swallowed two gulps of water, his eyes reddened as fear rippled through him. The kayak bobbed up to an upright position just as the shark opened its mouth to gnash and the waves rolled to the shores. The shark rushed across under the kayak to the other side of it. The scull was floating on the water. Dave stretched and grabbed it and paddled frantically. The shark followed suit, attacking the scull, as it rushed the scull, Dave lifted it up out of water in an arc across the kayak to the other side and paddled on, the shark rushed underneath the kayak to the other side to attack the scull. The kayak shuddered as the fin on the back of the shark grazed against it. Dave prayed silently that the beast wouldn't puncture the kayak and make a breakfast of him. A large wave rolled toward the banks sending the kayak high into the crest and pushed it forward onto the white sand beach. The shark lurked in the surf some few fathoms deep, eying its prey – Dave, sure that he wouldn't come back to the water at least now and certain that it could not attack him on the relatively dry surface, beachhead, else the hunter becomes the hunted. The shark turned and swam back into the deep ocean.

Dave saw the shark as it wagged its way back to the ocean deep, he breathed deeply in, sending moist clear air into his lungs and let out a deep sigh of relief. He placed the foldaway scull that he still clutched in his hands beside the kayak, and reached for the narrow roll of rug carpet and lifted it onto the wet beach sand and rolled it forward unfolding it. He stepped onto the rug and crouched forward over the kayak to deflate it. As the air sizzled out he looked nervously around, the beach was deserted and quite unlike the high decibel Copacabana beach. The prevailing sound in this white sand private beach was silence except for the roar of the wave and the claps in the surf. He unfastened the clips on the shaft of the scull and folded it. He placed it on the already deflated kayak sheet and folded the sheet around it and held it in place with a thick rubber band. With the first aid bag slung over his shoulder and the folded fitment under his armpit he stepped forward on the carpet, kicking it to further unroll it as he moved towards the beach house to avoid leaving any clue of fresh foot marks on the sandy shore, for the investigators to feed on.

He walked the length of the sandy beach on the rug carpet to the six-inch elevated boardwalk that stretched to the back of the house. From afar, the beige rug carpet looked a dirty stripe on the white sand beach. Dave bent forward and lifted the edge of the rug and rolled it pulling and rolling. He kept the rolled lot and the folded inflatable kayak propped on the boardwalk out of view of the house. Walking round to the front of the house, he reached for the key in the bag, his eyes darting around to see who was watching or listening, but there was no one. He slotted the key inside the keyhole of the mortise lock and turned but the lock didn't move, he turned it back and forth just as the locksmith had advised, and "click", the lock moved and he pushed the door, opening it. He stepped in but not before looking nervously around for any onlooker. He closed the door behind him. Calm and silence reigned and all sense of apprehension fell away and he strutted into the house as if he were the one who owned it. He stopped at the ground floor sitting room and looked it over before climbing the stairs taking the steps one at a time to the upper floor of the house. The upper floor pool was still and clam, he walked down the corridor toward the rooms, and then to the kitchen. It was a real cook's kitchen, well equipped. Elaine flashed to memory.

"Will she be coming? Better not," he thought.

The last time he came to the house with Elaine, she'd gone upstairs to the kitchen and opened the refrigerator and poured them two glasses of orange juice.

"I like orange juice," she'd said as she handed him one glass.

Dave opened the refrigerator and saw some packets of fruit drinks. He closed it and placed his first aid medical bag on the kitchen table. An idea flashed to his mind and he reached into the bag and fumbled for the anti-anxiety drugs he uses—Xanax, an overdose of Xanax sends anyone to sleep within minutes of consumption, Dave knows. He brought out the pack and took ten tablets of it and opened a compartment in the kitchen fitments and took out a teacup and a silver spoon. He placed the tablets in the cup and crushed them with the back of the spoon bowl and poured little water into the cup and stirred with the spoon mixing the solution. He reached and brought out the hypodermic syringe fitted with a hypodermic needle from the first aid bag. Placing the needle into the solution in the cup, he pulled the plunger, sucking in the solution. He brought out a pack of pure orange juice from the fridge. He punched the needle into the paper packet of the orange juice and injected the drug solution into the content of the pack. He shook the pack vigorously before replacing it into the refrigerator. The drug adds no colour, no taste or odour to its solutions and at that dose it can send anyone dozing within minutes of consumption. Dave put the cup and the spoon into the sink and washed three times with detergent to avoid any clue to any forensic test. Violent crimes are not common in this playground of the monied cariocas — Rio residents, so obviously there would be a vigorous investigation after completing his mission.

He dried the cup, spoon and the sink, and replaced them. He glanced at his wristwatch. It wouldn't be long before they arrived. He thought of where to hide when they arrived.

"The rooms?

"In the enormous walk-in wardrobe?"

"In the master bedroom?"

None of them," he decided.

"Best" will go straight to his wardrobe and may see

him behind the clothes and raise alarm. He must hide in a place where nobody will see him or rouse him for at least twenty minutes, an enough time for Elaine and whoever comes with them to unpack their bags and have a cup of orange juice and doze off. He thought of the scullery.

"Nice idea," he murmured and walked into the scullery. He looked around but there seemed nowhere to hide inside it. Then he walked over to the sink unit, and bent to pull open the cupboard underneath. He found a space large enough to contain him. He crouched, huddled himself into it and drew it closed.

"Comfortable enough to stay for thirty minutes," he thought.

He pulled the cupboard open and crawled out. He prepared the anaesthesia and fed the syringe and covered the hypodermic needle with its cover, and placed the first aid medical bag into the cupboard under the sink. He was ready. The house was so quiet he could hear his own breathing. The roar of waves was distant from inside the house, but the tide was rising.

CHAPTER 24
London, England

Evan and the four guys with him arrived early at the Covent Garden much like they obtained their premium opera tickets early using his wife's membership edge. His wife is a £90 annual member of the more than Nineteen Thousand Friends of Covent Garden. The concert was announced to be the last opera concert in Covent Garden before it closes down for a multi-million pound renovation. There is no doubt that Coach Cromwell will be present. There was a big crush in the theatre Bar. Evan and company scanned the crush in search of Coach Cromwell. The plot is simple. Locate him in the crush bar as he tries to enter the theatre, besiege him, show him the guns and if he wants to panic, spray the gas on him, knocking him out quietly, but most probably fear will seize him enough to quieten him. And in a low cold and coarse voice he will be told to accompany them to the outside and before he recovers from the shock and fear they must be outside the crush bar and inside the car. Take him to a safe place – anaesthetize him before doing the deed.

Mr. Cromwell opened the right side door of the white Range Rover Jeep for his wife and walked round the car to the owner's side where the driver held the door open for him. As he lifted his right leg up to climb into the vehicle, he felt a palpitation as the artery that empties blood into the ventricles – the heart's main pumping chambers – started to fibrillate. His heart started to race at about 160 beats per minuets, dizzying him. He gasped for air and then fell sidelong onto the marbled floor of the outer garage. His driver lifted him up into the car and they sped off to the hospital. The doctor was already waiting in the cardiac emergency room, standing like a demigod waiting to save the life of a worshiper against an intruding force. He fixed electrodes on Mr. Cromwell's chest and began to shock the heart back to normal rhythm, but to no avail. He administered a blood thinner called Warfarin. He tried again to shock it back to normal rhythm, but again no way. Suddenly, it appeared the heart had stopped entirely. The doctor looked at the monitor and noticed that the spikes that indicate pulse had diminished into tiny squiggles.

He pressed his hands on top of the electrodes, pushed and pressed to help to jumpstart the heart but Cromwell drifted into a deep sleep. The premium opera, MAN UTD, and the entire world spun without him for the next forty-five seconds until the electrical shocks revived the pumping of blood in his heart.

"He will stay six months on bed rest away from any kind of work to come back to total normalcy. Within this period he must enrol in mind-body medicine to learn meditation, yoga stance and breathing exercises," said the doctor to Mr. Cromwell's rather happy wife, happy that he was revived back to life. "But he will never work as a coach again," added the doctor.

"Being alive for me is enough," replied Mrs. Cromwell.

Mr. Cromwell had planned to retire in ten years but after years of high undulating emotional stress behind the white lines in front of the trainer's bench in the football pitches in high stake football duels, the unknown caught him and now made him a heart patient and would bench him forever from his most beloved job – conquering trophies. Just the way Mr. Cromwell benched players when they didn't prove their tuft, his heart had benched him for not caring enough for it even when he knew that heart problems were a hereditary trait. His father had died at the age of 50 years, of a sudden cardiac death, a detail that had been omitted on the genetic information and history that the MAN UTD football club obtained on him before signing his five year renewable contract.

Evan and his group stayed till the end of the concert but Cromwell didn't appear. They went home and reported to the Mob's Lieutenant Commander, Comrade Harvey. Harvey summoned the Mob intelligence officers to investigate the sudden truancy of Mr. Cromwell from his habitual premium opera concert attendance.

"Somebody must've sold the family off on this, somebody must've tipped Mr. Cromwell, it can't be coincidence, Mr. Cromwell can't afford to miss a premium opera concert, and the last before the Covent Garden closes for renovations for that matter. The traitor must be fished out and punished," charged Comrade

Harvey.

It would be six hours before London, European and American TV and radio stations announced that Coach Cromwell had a heart attack and would never work as a coach again.

CHAPTER 25
Angra dos Reis, Brazil

Dave heard the buzzing sound of a helicopter in the distance, the noise increasing with each passing second and becoming deafening as the Robson R44 helicopter hovered above the house and perched on the rooftop helipad that Dave had not noticed. Dave went and curled into the cupboard underneath the sink unit and drew it close. He heard the faint footsteps of the new arrivals as they entered the house. There were three different footsteps that Dave believed must be that of the cook, and maybe Elaine or any other house help. The masculine footsteps, Dave guessed, were those of the pilot.

" 'Best'? Could he have piloted the helicopter to this place, without an instructor? Most probably, yes," Dave thought.

He waited. The cupboard somehow reminded him of the coffin he had laid in overnight in Brixton, London, in wait for death, as he'd believed then. Here, he was once again inside a small box-like compartment in wait, but this time not for his death, nor torture, but to deliver the Mob's wish. The two feminine steps approached the kitchen, then paused. Dave heard the jangling of keys and then a clink as the key turned in the lock minutes later. He heard footsteps go into the kitchen, followed by others. He heard the scraping sound of a chair as someone pulled the kitchen dining-chair across the floor. He heard the refrigerator door open then closed. He heard a cupboard opened and the clinking sound of glass cups then the cupboard closed. He listened to two female voices as they discussed domestic gossips. One of the voices was unmistakably Elaine's.

She'd come with them finally.

"Thank God I'd drugged the orange juice, her favourite fruit drink," he thought, and waited. He heard the other voice say thanks to Elaine. Probably she'd given her a glass of the orange juice. And fifteen minutes later the kitchen was quiet, though Dave never heard any footsteps walking out, he waited ten more minutes. He heard a faint ring of a bell.

"Best" was calling their attention, but there came no movements from the kitchen, or in the house. Two minutes later the bell chimed again, yet no movements. Dave became sure the drug was in action, the two ladies were fast asleep. He drew the cupboard open and crawled out as the bell rang again. He pulled out the first aid bag, slung it over this shoulder and drew his gun from its waist holster. He tiptoed out the scullery into the kitchen and into the corridor to the master bedroom. Standing by the foyer doorway, he waited for a sound to clue him in as to the position of "best" in the room, but no sound, no movement came. He knew he had to move, he can't stand there for a long time. Then the bell rang again in the kitchen. Dave didn't know how long he stood in wait but the bell awakened him. It was quite on time. As he stepped into the room, "best" would obviously think it was one of the maids who had come to answer his call. He moved into the room, gun in a shoot-ready position. "Best" was standing before the full-length mirror in the room. On hearing the footsteps through the doorway, he turned around before Dave's image appeared in the mirror. He squinted at Dave, assessing him. Dave looked into his eyes – they were totally devoid of fear or appeal for pity, but instead filled with surprise and confidence, the confidence of a person who was used to being loved, respected and praised.

"Best" was too surprised to be afraid. His life and success were moulded and formed on his ability to pass through the barriers of adversaries, waiting adversaries. He was preparing in his mind to dribble this gun brandishing stranger but each time the instinct wanted to push, a restraining chill went down his spine. He'd never dribbled a man with a short gun and an index finger held against the trigger. This was not football, obviously not a ball on the green grass otherwise he would've put the ball through his legs that were held 35 cm apart. Dave had said nothing yet.

The atmosphere crackled with tension. Dave made two steps forward and "best" curled his fingers into a fist and tightened them and then tighter as if that would stop Dave from approaching further.

"No smart moves," Dave growled and made two more steps forward. "Best" saw the determination and violence in his eyes.

"He certainly comes from the Mafia stock," thought "Best", and fear descended on him. He kept breathless and still as tension rippled through him.

"On your stomach!" Dave ordered.

"Best" felt something rise up inside him, refusing to accept and obey the order. The instinct lurking beneath his now fear soured face was trying to refuse what Dave was imposing, he wanted to spring onto Dave, but the restraining chill came again.

"The man wouldn't hesitate to use the toy in his hand," the restraining mind reminded him.

"On your stomach, I said," Dave repeated.

"Don't let me use this," he added, waving the short gun.

"Best" knew that there was only one way out — he was besieged and he had to obey his orders, the asshole's orders. Reluctantly he bent forward and dropped on his stomach. Dave reached his bag for the cuffs. He bounded "best's" ankles and his wrists before blindfolding and gagging him. As he brought out the syringe to anaesthetize him, he looked him over, he was looking at the world's ex-best footballer, 'cause he knew that the cycle of football would soon be spinning without him and the world football body would soon be searching for the next world's best. It would be very long before he smiled heartily again in his life, that broad hearty smile. The last time he, Dave, and the world saw him smile broadly in the football pitch was when he scored the lone goal for his team in their penultimate match. It was his last smile in the world of football as a player and never again, never would he . . .

Dave bent forward, pushed the needle into the vein in his knee and pushed down the plunger anaesthetizing him. With the scalpel, Dave visited the tendons and ligaments in the kneecap region. He completed the rest of the deed and placed fresh cotton wool over the cuts and held them tightly in place with ligatures. The job was done. He packed his lot into the first aid bag and hurried out the room towards the kitchen and peeped in: the two maids were still sleeping.

"Everything is alright," he murmured and started towards the stairs. He descended the steps rapidly onto the ground floor sitting room and walked to the front door and stepped into the open and scurried across the pavement. Standing on the edge of the pavement, he stretch to take the folded lot he had left propped against the pavement riser. He unrolled the rug carpet across the white sand beach to the water edge where he inflated the kayak rapidly and folded the carpet from inside the kayak, pulling as he folded it. The tide had ebbed but each peak of surf still broke with a clap, weak though. As he paddled to the heavy foliage shore, he threw the blood-soaked cotton wool into the water. On seeing blood in the water, the sharks swarm towards the blood, foraging for the prey. Meanwhile, Dave paddled forward to the motorboat. Minutes later, he was speeding across the high sea back to Rio de Janeiro.

CHAPTER 26
Rio de Janeiro, Brazil

Dave settled his hotel bill and submitted his suite key to the receptionist and waved down a taxi in front of the hotel.

"Airport," he told the driver as he settled into the back seat of the 1990 Ford sedan.

He would've loved to stay and witness the Carnival, the much orchestrated Rio Carnival, but "best" was a mega star in Brazil, whose presence in the streets got people trampled, and for whom people cried and screamed out in deep emotion and whose acts and per-formances people venerated as if there had never been another footballer before him, as if he had personally invented football. For such a person, people will skin one alive at the flimsiest of suspicion. They will find it utterly wrong to be deprived of him and the adrenal highs and lows he knows to give them. Here in Brazil, where football is like a religion and football cracks are demigods. Fans will be happy to die killing and trying to kill just like an Islamic soldier to a Jihad. He must leave before any eyebrows of suspicion would be raised to his direction. The whole thing was foolproof, though, but you never know.

"Voce vai embora? Sem assistir Carnival?" asked the driver.

"No I'm not going home, I'm going to Bahia, Nordest to witness the Carnival there," Dave lied.

"Bahia tamben e muito bom, muito mulher," said the driver.

"Yes," said Dave.

"Mulher Brazilero e o melhor de mundo, condorda?" asked the driver.

"Yes, Brazilian women are the best in the world, I agree with you," replied Dave.

"Ehh! Gringo, gringo. Mulher e bom ne?" said the driver.

"Yes, women are good," replied Dave.

"Qual companhaerea que voce vai pegar?" asked the

driver as he turned into the departure lane to the airport.

"Varig," said Dave.

Dave came down the car and paid him off.

Varig had no flight to London that night, and the British Airways passengers were checking in. Dave went to the British Airways ticketing counter and presented his Varig ticket. His was a transferable and endorsable ticket.

"You are going to London? Yes?" asked the lady behind the counter. "Varig ticket?" she added.

Dave nodded his yes, praying silently that she didn't refuse him.

The lady perked on the computer keyboards and nodded in approval as the confirmation data on the tickets scrolled down the computer screen. She perked more keys, changing what needed to be changed and corrected.

"Any baggage?" she asked.

"Only hand luggage," replied Dave.

She handed Dave his ticket jacket and a boarding pass. Dave picked up the lot and happily went to join the boarding queue. He pushed his passport and boarding pass through the hatch into the immigration cage to the moustached Immigration man. The man opened the passport and crosschecked some data and pushed it back to him.

"Tchau!" he greeted.

"Tchau! Tchau!" replied Dave and moved quickly forward to the x-ray conveyor belt. He dropped his bag on it and the machine hummed into life pushing it across. Dave crossed the scan gate and collected his bag from the conveyor belt and headed for boarding. He paused at the tube, looked over his shoulder.

"Tchau! Tchau!" he said to the lady standing by the edge of the tube.

"Tchau!" replied the lady with a broad professional smile. She was the last Brazilian Dave spoke to on Brazilian soil.

The plane roared along the runway, hopped into the warm evening Rio air to airborne.

"Mission very well accomplished," murmured Dave and crossed his self in gratitude to the saints. It was his first international gangster mission and it was a success.

"God bless Rio de Janeiro," he mused, glancing at

the watch strapped on his left wrist. The time was 9:15 p.m., the same time he flew out of Heathrow airport for Brazil. Everything was alright. He stretched his legs and adjusted the headrest of his seat as the cautionary take-off signals went off.

Chapter 27
London, England

It was 8:30 p.m. and Tom had eaten his dinner with his wife, Kate, and listened to the evening news: to the BBC World Report, and read the evening tabloid. All was normal and well in his household. Kate heard the scrape as Tom pulled a chair and sat before the computer, fired it on and looked on as the Euro fell against the dollar, and the island dollar's value didn't blink. The pound was steady and the South African Rand's appreciated against the US dollar following the news of gold value appreciation. Tom highlighted quote, venturing into the $1.5 trillion a day world of foreign currency trade through the World Wide Web. He typed in Island Dollars to place a U$5M order with just U$50,000 down on his on-line dollar currency trading account, utilizing the broker's loan and waited for his offer to be accepted, the price pipped as he waited. He looked at the new price, paused and pondered, then accepted it.

Kate came into the room, looking at the screen from over Tom's shoulders.

"Hmm, you are betting on new Island dollars? Remember you haven't got a good life insurance policy, 'cause Eddy the cat and the dog will need it to carry on with life," she said.

Tom laughed.

"I've got the formula," boasted Tom. "I listened to the world news. The loan everybody had believed the Islanders would default on, and plug its currency into new lows was paid. The island nation didn't package it into the Brady Bond backed by the US Treasury bonds that would've given it another thirty days' grace before it would be formally declared a default. The currency is now in the clear and tradable. The Island Congress also voted last week to dollarize their economy and their central bank has approved the plan and the currency by tomorrow will be utterly strengthened when the rate at which to dollarize will be fixed, and before the normal trading starts I must've made my profits," said Tom, taking a swig from the beer bottle on the table beside the computer keyboard.

"It is not because of its position in the world currency hierarchy, but I was only imagining how you do business with capitalization in hundreds of thousands and millions of dollars and make profits in tens of hundreds. Besides, I think it's risky to do business with an economy on the verge of dollarization," said Kate.

Tom conducted his transaction at the rate of one US dollar to 500 Island dollars. He knew very well that it was a very risky transaction but he also knew that the same factors that made it risky also made it a very lucrative transaction depending on how things swing. He was very sure that by tomorrow the Island dollars would appreciate against the US dollars as the rate would be fixed to allow enough dollars in the hands of the Islanders to start off the dollarization era, since the central bank would lose control of much of the Island's monetary policy. The rate must definitely be lower than 500, most probably at about 300 Island dollars to one US dollar. And he, Tom, would make his killing. He stayed in front of his computer, watching the prices pip as the night aged. Suddenly the Island dollars started rising against the dollar, and in the next two hours he had made $1,000 before nodding to sleep, leaving the computer running.

He woke up with a start the next morning. It was all a dream. He was dreaming of his good old days of day trading.

CHAPTER 28

The British Airways flight touched ground at the Heathrow airport at 6:30 a.m. and Dave alighted from the aircraft happy and confident. He collected the morning daily newspaper from a newspaper stand in the arrival hall. All the newspapers had it on the headlines.

"The Manchester Saga!" said the Daily Times.

"Mysterious Home Injuries at MAN UTD rank and file," read the Herald.

"The Butchery Fun at MAN UTD," said the Mirror.

Bradley got languidly out of bed and collected his morning daily from the house mailbox. He read the headlines and smiled. He went into the sitting room and perused the topics.

Coach Cromwell had not been blinded but he got an

equally restraining hit.

"Could it be by the Mob? Or is it a natural occurrence?" pondered Bradley. "But these people could be efficient," he mused of the Mob.

He fired his computer and checked the MAN UTD share price. It had already dipped from its upper three digits level to a low two digits point. He moistened his lips with his tongue and a proud smile creased his cheek.

Tom woke up in the morning a poor man, his share holding with the MAN UTD as good as worthless. He'd never been more wiped out nor more deeply in debt and his house was the only valuable security he had.

In the evening, the share prices of the MAN UTD had come down to a much lower two digits point. The management of Manchester United Football Club bought back some shares to shore up its share prices but to no avail. Bradley waited until the next day before delivering the stock to a buyer. The spread was £9 m and he submitted half of it, £4.5m to Johnny Bandit's Mob and kept his £4.5m. Johnny and the Mob were most delighted. It was such a clean deal, nobody died, no drugs sold nor young girls ferried across borders into prostitution. Johnny and the Mob reserve a great respect and admiration for Bradley and their friendship with him will forever be.

Betsky received the money, $250,000 in US dollars because she had a foreign passport. The money was packed in a briefcase provided by the bank, and she made straight to Daniskov's house. Daniskov opened the briefcase and the crisp smell of newly minted cash hit his nostrils. He touched the notes on the surface, his pupils dilating. He closed the briefcase quickly and looked around nervously as if to make sure no thief was marauding in the vicinity.

Betsky noted the momentary lapse of equilibrium in his comportment exerted by the sight of the money.

"Normal," she thought.

She had often wondered before now which was stronger, the power of money or the power of love.

Daniskov smiled sheepishly, exposing his vodka stained teeth and gums, a very distant homing looks in his eyes. He could imagine the neurologist performing the new experimental treatment on him to regain his mobility. As the neurologist collected immature spinal cord cells, placed them in a Petri dish inside an incubator, stuffed it with nutrients and adjusted the supply of heat and oxygen and the cells began their regeneration process. He reimplanted the cells in the gap of his severed spinal cord and then he, Daniskov, waited for two weeks as the cells made their reconnections with the nerve fibres of the numerous cells of the spinal cord to become functional, allowing the passage of commands and orders through the neurons and synapses from the part of the brain that controls mobility.

"Ready!" he mused and pushed forward to get up but the order from his brain wasn't delivered to his leg muscles, rather, he felt a tickling sensation in the inner small of his back. It was only a daylight dream, his imagination based on what the neurologist had told him he could do for him if there was enough money to embark on the treatment, an experimental treatment. It had been a long time since he was told this by the neurologist. It was a dead dream that was awakening in his conscious mind by the mere sight of the cash, a quarter of a million US dollars, the dowry from his first wife to divorce his second wife to save their son from going to war in Chechnya.

Daniskov had told Betsky to bring the money but he

didn't mean it, he was only trying to dismiss her subtly, but what he thought to be a very good way of telling her "no" had turned into a reality. He'd never in his wildest of imagination known that Betsky could weave such an amount of money together. It was like a Hollywood fiction, magic, western magic, American wonder. And the magic may be capable of resolving his confinement to the wheel chair. He looked slowly up at Betsky and then at the briefcase.

"God must be a westerner," he thought.

"Koytov is a good boy, he won't go to war. If the Caucasian republics want to secede, it's for them to do so and not for Koy to stop them. The Russian army can win the war without Koytov. I'm sure they won't miss him," said Daniskov.

This amount of money together in cash was the next greatest surprise Daniskov had witnessed in his life after the surprise of the collapse of the Soviet power.

"With this much, one can even buy Chechnya and call off the war," he thought.

"Is the west this good?" asked Daniskov.

Betsky looked him over and kept mute.

Chapter 29
Moscow, Russia

"Betsky was here while you were at the office," said Daniskov to Nerhcy, his wife.

"Always when I'm at work. She must know that this is no longer her home. You are no longer her husband. You've told her how it's like, so why come here again, to plead? Selfish bitch!" said Nerhcy.

"I'm sure she knows," replied Daniskov. "She brought the money. Complete," he added.

"Eh? She brought the money? How much did you say you told her the other day? Half a million dollars?" asked Nerhcy.

"No, a quarter of a million dollars," corrected Daniskov.

"And she brought it?" asked Nerhcy, a mocking

smile creasing her face.

"Yes, she did, no jokes," replied Daniskov.

"Sure it's not a fake cheque?" asked Nerhcy.

"It's cash, Nerhcy, raw cash, in American dollars."

Nerhcy paused, gazed at Daniskov.

"You must be joking," she said and started going away.

"Nerhcy, I'm not joking," said Daniskov.

"Yes?" she answered, turning.

"Bring the briefcase in my wardrobe," said Daniskov. "Careful, it's heavy."

Nerhcy went into the room, pulled the wardrobe open and scrambled among the clothes and found the briefcase and pulled it out by its handle and made for the sitting room, leaving the wardrobe open. She placed it on its belly on the centre table in the sitting room.

"Open!" said Daniskov. "ooo left, 111 right is the combination," he added.

Nerhcy crouched over the briefcase and arranged the digits to the said combination and opened. She gazed at the neatly arranged cash and then looked slowly up at Daniskov and back at the cash.

"Is it real money?" she asked finally. "I hope it is,

it's real, she can't be that daft, can she?"

"Of course not," said Daniskov.

"How come all the cash? Half a million dollars," said Nerhcy. "I mean a quarter of a million dollars," she corrected.

"The west, capitalism. She's always got the Darwinian instinct. She went to the west where her instinct matches with the economy, the free market economy as it is called, the type we are embracing now, that's how come," said Daniskov.

"A quarter of a million dollars. The west," Nerhcy said. "That's where the world is, eh?"

A pause.

"The world is in Europe but ends in America," replied Daniskov finally.

"And now?" asked Nerhcy. "Will you divorce me?" she added.

"I ask you, Nerhcy. And now? What do we do?" said Daniskov.

Nerhcy looked at him and then at the open briefcase. She walked over to the window, peeped through the louvers of the blind then turned to Daniskov.

"It is a lot of money, Dan," she said, folding her arms

on her chest. "Too much money," she added, and started to pace the sitting room.

"A quarter of the money can get you walking again, so the doctor once said – the experimental treatment. With half of it, we can have our own McDonald's restaurant. Another quarter can buy us a car and a bigger house and our daily dose of vodka. It is a big money and besides Koytov is not the war type. After all this war has been going on since 1783 when the Caucasus was still dominated by tribal authorities like the Chechens and the Inguish in the days of Catherine the Great who declared Caucasus a Russian province and a bloody war against conquest ensued and lasted until 1859. But Russian troops still maintained presence on Caucasus soil until 1917 when they became an autonomous republic under the Bolsheviks. But in the '40's during the second World War, the Caucasus lend support to the invading Third Reich army and this infuriated Stalin who reinvaded the Caucasus and expelled a lot of their leaders to central Asia. After World War II and the death of Stalin in 1956, the exiled Chechnya and Inguish leaders were allowed to return home. During this period, Saudi Arabia began to spread the Wahabi Islamist influence into the Caucasus. During Prestorika and Glasnost and the eventual collapse of the Soviet Union, President Boris Yeltsin declared all Russia's subjects autonomous and Chechnya parliament declared national independence which didn't appease Russia and especially Russia's interest for the Caucasus oil fields and hence this war. All this, which has been going on for the past 21 decades couldn't be resolved by Koytov's presence or absence in the Russian army line-up, he doesn't have much to contribute. We can waive the war for him.

"What do you say?" asked Nerhcy, pausing to look at Daniskov.

"I think so too," Daniskov said, nodding approvingly.

"So?" said Nerhcy.

Daniskov shrugged his shoulders resignedly.

"When?" asked Nerhcy.

"Any day, today, tomorrow, or next. She wants it quickly before Koytov receives an official draft notice," said Daniskov.

"Today is already out of the question, it's already five o'clock. The divorce office closes at five. Tomorrow you file the papers," said Nerhcy.

"No, you file it," replied Daniskov.

"No, not me, Dan, you file it," replied Nerhcy.

"No, you do it," insisted Daniskov.

"Look Dan, nobody knows the game we are playing. How could they know we will get back together immediately after the war? It will be so callous of me to divorce you while you are on the wheelchair and jobless. That is what everybody would think about me. But if you file the divorce paper it looks more like it's real, that I'm probably giving you a hell of a lot of trouble and you cannot take it any longer and you kicked me out. Thank God you have a grown-up son who will take care of you," said Nerhcy.

Daniskov looked slowly away, breathed gently but deeply in.

"Okay, you win," he said, looking back at her. "I will file the papers tomorrow," he said.

CHAPTER 30

Betsky wasn't any less surprised and agape at the stash of cash sent by Bradley within such a short notice, less than a month. One thing she was very certain of was that Bradley hadn't got a sixth of this cash before she left for Moscow.

She had often felt so connected to Bradley, her husband, but at the moment, though she was very happy, that after all her son would be saved from going to war in the Chechnya. But she felt so disconnected with Bradley. She had always known him to have an instinct for making money, plotting, executing and reaping his yield like most modern men. But this much, this sudden, was frightening if impressive. It made her feel incapacitated, after years of spousal life with her man, she thought she's known his full potential but alas she was wrong. She was noticing a new hype in her man, a new ability, a new compartment of his ability, a hidden one. She felt resentment for herself because she would've loved to find it out herself and not for Bradley to show her without details. If she couldn't deduce her husband whom could she deduce? The same happened with the man she spent half her life with – Daniskov. She'd never believed that Daniskov would charge her money to sign the divorce papers to save their son's life. Could it be that she is not woman enough to read, assimilate and deduce her men or is it that men have these inner selves that cannot be communicated to, irrespective of their daily activities and closeness with their women?

"You never know a man well enough to deduce and fill in the spaces for him," her mother had once told her. "The person you best know is yourself."

Betsky is never at home with a man who is very clever with money, smart and fashionable. The simple reason is that they are often very hard to manage. But Bradley had never been hard to explore nor had he been pretending. Whatever it is, the combination of money and fashion is so brash, though she likes what money buys.

Things like real freedom, that's why she immigrated to the west after all. And today, almost a decade later, she's back home in Moscow to have a piece of it, freedom bought with money, for her son. Bradley has always been happy with his work, researching, but he's often complained how much one needs to save and strive in other to continue in the laboratory and how much it could be uncompensating sometimes, especially when at the end, if the research becomes fruitless, money and years wasted and hopes shattered.

Betsky knew that Bradley never liked loans and doesn't borrow. But if so, how come this money magic of his?

Could it be crime like most quick riches? Betsky never liked shady business or shady men. They keep one in constant contemplation and atimes on the defensive. You never know their next move. But in all, Betsky should be giving gratitude to God and Bradley and not probe him, after all he couldn't have committed the crime or whatever on a selfish interest any more than Daniskov had demanded a quarter of a million dollars to accept divorce offer to save Koytov from dying in the snow-capped Chechnya mountains defending Moscow.

Even if it is a crime that Bradley had committed to assemble the cash, he is not a criminal but rather a professional who slipped on a crime cloak to pull over a hurdle. Besides, what she herself is aiding and abetting here in Moscow is a crime in itself. Bradley had once told her that nobody is so clean, only that some people are dirtier than others. There is this little criminal in everyone but while some are so bloody red collared, others are blue, brown and some are white. Everybody is sort of a criminal operating on different sides of the law. If it was crime that Bradley committed then she, Betsky, was responsible for awakening it, something he's been restraining from being born, which is so deeply embedded in him. In that case, they are both criminals operating on different sides of the law.

Chapter 31
London, England

All was sour in Tom's household. He was poor and deeply in debt. "But it's going to be all right," he murmured as he sat in his sitting room dreaming up quids in to resolve his financial quagmire. He would create an auction web site and advertise a non-refundable ticket for a two months maternity delivery holidays on Mir-like spacecraft. Mir was the world's longest served Russian made spacecraft. He would advertise for the first child to be born in space. The tickets would only be viable for couples, with the wife at seven months of gestation. He would bid on the auction to drag up the price. He would call Teddy to bid from Paris. Paul could've helped from Los Angeles. Paul was a good guy for this kind of swindle but the last time Tom spoke with him he'd told him that he'd been dismissed from the bank where he worked and was facing charges from prosecutors and securities officials for insider trading. He'd once passed him, Tom, information about a merger, information he got eavesdropping into the discussions of the bank executives, taking cups of coffee, tea, water to them in the conference room table, collecting back the empty cups and bringing refills. He'd heard them mention the market sectors, headquarters and price range of stocks and locations of companies. Ever curious, Paul had used the tidbits of information to ransack Websites to find the names of the companies. He'd passed the information to friends, including Tom. Tom made £400,000 trading on the stocks. The spread from that trade had impressed Kate so much.

"Poor Paul, hope he wins," thought Tom.

He would also advertise the auction of noble titles, like Baron, Lady, Sir, Lord. He would tease his would-be victims that the titles confers lots of social and business benefits worldwide, and that they are fully recognized under English law and could be used in one's name and could be passed to their heirs and also could be used in one's documents like passport, identity, and credit cards. He would flatter them on the proud history of the previous holders of the titles and places where they abound. He would remind them that only individuals with impeccable integrity will be accepted, because the titles would form part of British history and tradition millenniums to come. £100,000 per title is a good price.

He would make sure that whoever won the bidding was the client whom he took the initiative in clicking so that in the case of comebacks that would ensue, the case would be settled in the client's country's court and as such the English courts will not have jurisdiction to the case nor extradite him to the said country.

"Noble titles must be obtained on merits, and not for sale," he thought in defence.

He knew enough alibi peddlers to help in convincing the probing Thomas' when they crosscheck data, especially off line.

"It will work out," he mused.

He paused in thought on remembering that he'd promised himself not to mess with crime again. The yard is so ugly and sad a place. He reached for his Bible and opened at Romans 12:12 and read:

"Rejoice in hope, be patient in tribulation and persevere in prayer."

"Persevere in prayer," he repeated out loud and opened up yet another page at Second Corinthians 12:10 and read:

"Therefore I take pleasure in infirmities, in reproaches, in necessities, in persecution, in distresses for Christ's sake for when I am weak then I am strong."

Kate pondered deeply as she unpacked her belongings in Beatrice's apartment east of London. Something was strange about Tom's reaction to her divorce request. She'd expected a surprise hazy pleading look in his eyes urging her to stay on, that it's gonna be alright, while she refused and laid her accusations, but not the upfront confidence that was shining in Tom's eyes, his stoic acceptance. Obviously she no longer dazzles him. She was sure that he's got nothing left but what thickens him was what she couldn't figure out. It was the first time a man showed no emotional concern at being dumped by her, a fallen guy for that matter, well, they've always been fallen guys because Kate had never left a man in his strength. She hated the feeling that grew up inside her, a feeling that she's at loss but there was no doubt that she wanted nothing else from Tom, what she'd desired in him is spent and gone, though the muse of stock picking might revisit him again probably after much toiling but now she wants another sucker.

Thoughts kept tumbling down Tom's mind.

Max suddenly came to mind, Maxwell the millionaire, his childhood friend.

"Let's try Max first," he murmured to himself, and stretched to reach the phone.

CHAPTER 32

Bradley screened the faces of the passengers as they streamed out into the arrival hall of the Gatwick airport. He saw Betsky and a teenager with the first dawn of youth on his face, walking beside her as they approached. Betsky looked forward and saw Bradley impeccably dressed. She strutted towards him and Bradley moved to her, grinning with his arms wide stretched. They embraced, kissed and held each other in a warm affection. Betsky caught a strong whiff of his fragrant French perfume. She looked up into his face, his jaw white from a recent shave. Bradley bent and kissed her again and offered her a single rose flower.

Betsky smelt it, kissed it, her smile widened. "You are unrestrainingly irresistible, Brad," she said, looking into his eyes and then slowly down to his feet. The ensemble is completely new and different, none of the relatively shabby suites in his wardrobe, the real researchers suits. This is a designer's suit, a new Bradley with fey suit, perfumed, shaven and surer. So much is lit in him. Betsky had always known a latent aesthetics in Bradley, and today she's seen it born.

Koytov stood beside them wearing a pleasant smile. Bradley looked his way and Betsky followed his gaze.

"Guess who he is?" said Betsky.

"The smiling eyes, the sensual mouth is from his mother, Betsky. I've never seen Betsky's ex-husband, but surely the rest of Koytov must be from Betsky's ex-husband or a mixture of him and Betsky," thought Bradley.

"Can't be your new-found young love," he said, stretching a hand to Koytov. "Must be Koytov," he added as Koytov took his hand for a shake.

"Are you alright, dear?" he said.

"Hallo," Koytov said with an eastern lilt.

Bradley noticed the ring on the tip of his tongue as it lolled out like the tongue of a wild reptile. Bradley detests body piercing and body jewellery but he knows that he, Koytov, is an adolescent and must've been driven by vogue. He thought of the pains he must've endured to have his tongue pierced, the allergy he might get from the low quality jewellery, teeth fracture, the numbness and other et cetera things that might ail him from this youthful act of vanity.

"You will enjoy England. It is peaceful here, no wars," said Bradley.

"I'd brought him to live with us, to enjoy what the British society and economy has to offer," said Betsky.

Bradley walked them to the car park. Betsky looked around for the white 1989 BMW, but Bradley led them to a waiting black Mercedes limo. The chauffeur held the door open for them and they entered into the stretch limo. The chauffeur pushed the door shut, got behind the wheels and fired the engine, engaged the floor gear and rolled out but not before glancing over his shoulder at the beaming couple to make sure they were alright before closing the glass screen hatch.

"Your driver?" Betsky whispered into Bradley's ear.

"Yes," said Bradley, "Just to bring you home today," he added.

Back home, the chauffeur hung around for another

two hours before leaving. Betsky noticed that so much had changed within so little a time. The money Bradley had earned was far beyond his known source of income and any crime she'd imagined he committed.

The furniture in the living room had been replaced with a more aesthetic set of furniture. There were new carpets, and new books in the library. His laboratory was now fully equipped with sophisticated machines, even the pool had been realigned. Bradley explained to her that it had been relined with special techniques that work against bacteria and one can leave the pool without taking a wash. The pool had water massage features.

It was the next day after the Sunday lunch that Betsky asked Bradley about the sudden changes.

"What is happening, Brad?" she asked.

"About?" replied Bradley.

"The money you sent me, how come about it?" she continued.

Bradley smiled, he knows quite well that she'd have to be inhuman not to be confused at this overnight plush changes.

"I short sold some stock and the spread was substantial," Bradley said.

"What stock?" asked Betsky.

"Entertainment stock."

"Which?"

"MAN UTD football club stock," replied Bradley.

Betsky's curiosity was alit — the butchery at MAN UTD 'rank and file' — the Mirror headline. 'Could it have been Bradley? No, it couldn't be. Is she learning more about this man than she'd wanted to? But he is her husband so she ought to. No, it can't be, it must be a coincidence. But why an entertainment stock when he knows so much about science and technology stocks,' tumbled her thoughts.

Betsky was looking straight into his eyes now, searching for quivers and telltale signs of lies, but the confidence in his eyes was well rested. Bradley saw the fear, the doubt in her eyes. Betsky knew he saw them as she looked on at him. She knew how bad it is to show one's husband you don't trust him, though it doesn't mean you don't love him, because love can survive in the absence of trust and trust in the absence of love. Trust is respect and that's even worse because Bradley loves respect which he equates to space, not physical space though.

Two days later Bradley received an invitation to attend a party, a sleepover party at the London Sheraton Hotel to be hosted by Johnny Bandit. Bradley had not wanted to attend the party. He doesn't need the closeness, but it would be churlish to turn down the invitation. However he went to the party with Betsky. It was a fabulous party attended by the cream of the London society. If there were any Mr. and Mrs. No-Name at the party, it was Mr. and Mrs. Bradley. Johnny came to greet Bradley and Betsky thirty minutes after they arrived.

"Johnny Bandit," he said in a rich deep voice, introducing himself to Betsky.

"Johnny Bandit," thought Betsky. She felt her breath cut. What are they doing around people like this, near Johnny Bandit. Bradley had told her the host is a friend he'd recently met. A man so perversely powerful that a word of order from him could make trains collide and bombs explode and people get kidnapped.

Johnny stayed a while with them before leaving, flanked by three bodyguards. The party was good but Betsky spent most of the night watching people and ruminating.

CHAPTER 33
Sheraton Hotel
London, England

Back in the hotel suite, Betsky continued in thought. She knows that character must not always be judged by the company one keeps, and she knows that Bradley had not lied when he told her he'd borrowed and short-sold some entertainment stock. Though she doubts if he'd told it straight from the shoulder, she will respect his space, his privacy. It is the very type of space that Bradley always demand from friends, and besides it's better that she, Betsky, knows nothing further than the periphery so that she doesn't become an accomplice, in case of any comebacks. But the connection is obvious – the football club stock, the chopped off sinews and kneecaps, the heart attack and the way it was all narrated in the tabloids, the overnight swollen bank account and a sleepover party in the Sheraton Hotel with Johnny Bandit as the host.

But to what extent was Bradley involved, is what Betsky hasn't really yet deciphered. But she is sure Bradley did business with the Mob only to pander to her problems.

"Poor Brad," she thought. She felt a sob growing in her throat and swallowed to suppress it.

It is very flattering to see the extent to which Bradley can go to see that her pride and interest is not hurt, to see that she is happy. She's always known that he loves her immensely, but . . . , she broke into a sob. She put her both palms on his cheeks and kissed him.

"I love you too, Brad," she crooned sniffingly. She stroked him, propping herself on the bed on her left elbow and watched Bradley as his breath deepened and he drifted into a deep sleep, lying innocently and vulnerable on the hotel suite bed as the ballroom fleeted through her mind, The serious and ambitious faces, the wide catchy and winsome smiles of the people, all bad people, none of them liking the next any bit as much as they pretended to, though this is not unusual among people engaged in high voltage life. But this type of company and life is not what she wants in life for herself, husband and family.

Researching is good for him and he has what it takes, though researching is a very torturous profession and requires tremendous patience and tolerance, it is a prestigious means of livelihood and colleagues respect and adore one another. Betsky knows that it is only expedient, his involvement with the Mob, because as a typical American, Bradley had done what it takes to resolve their problem, rather than wanting to do it the way it has always been done by which time Koytov might've been slain in the rugged terrain of the Chechnya.

"Thumbs up, Brad," she mused.

She closed her eyes and prayed that deception and greed, which assume different guises, don't get into his head and pull him deeper into crime and involvement with the Mob. This one time is one too many.

The concrete evidence is lacking though, but wild hypothesis is not much required to adduce that thinking up and selling the plot to the Mob must've been Bradley's contribution, otherwise, there is no other viable contribution he could have weighed in to partake in sharing the bounty. He couldn't have participated in the hitting. She knows he is not that violent. Otherwise, . . . for he that loves silver shall not be satisfied with silver nor he that loves abundance be satisfied with increase. Betsky reached and stroked his hair from the temple backwards in admiration. It's not as if she is afraid of change and dreams, she'd always wanted them, welcomed and embraced them and even toiled to create them, but change and dreams that are worthwhile, not going from a normal tranquil life to a rancorous one, to a life of high voltage risk. She dozed off, ruminating.

* * *

She opened her eyes to a slight knock on the door. Bradley was still sleeping. She crept out of bed quietly, careful not to stir a noise to wake him.

She opened the door and the waiter wheeled the tea wagon across the doorway into the room.

"Good morning madam," he said without looking into her face.

He left the tea wagon beside the dining table, turned and made for the exit, closing the door quietly behind him. Betsky went back to the bedroom, standing by the edge of the bed she watched Bradley breathe in and out in his sleep, his face handsome and innocent. She silently wished that he would remain innocent, the same stately face that walked up to her table in the pub, drew the seat opposite hers and sat down unexcused on a day she left her house with a sense of occasion. That day, her daily horoscopic guide had predicted that she would meet a very interesting gentleman whom she would never be tired of loving and learning about. It has been the only prediction of her horoscopic life that has come true.

"No offence, madam, but I'm not just a sucker for long black hair," Bradley had said smilingly. "But I'm also a sucker for fine long legs and slight squinted blue eyes. I'm a sucker for a looker like you," he added.

Betsky looked up at him, smiled and shook her head sideways, looked up at him again, this time sizing him up. She knew he was describing her features and she was happy he didn't exaggerate, though she didn't like his patronizing manner, but she didn't give a damn 'cause most men are like that, sexist. And if one should resent men based on their sexist attitudes, then . . . . It is part of the male ego.

Betsky didn't know if he really was a sucker. Because jokes apart, she really needed a sucker to tide her over the throes of the western cut-throat crunch she met in London. She was only two months old in the city of London on that day, almost a decade ago.

"Then buy us a ticket and book us a suite for April first for a two weeks holidays in the cruise ship Residensea or Mir," Betsky had replied, a Soviet upper class joke in a mocking admiration of western lavish and loud style of living, and in mockery of the Soviet spaceship Mir that rumours said will be transformed into a space hotel. She had said it to tow him along his line of humour.

"Oh, sure, April first, a good day for suckers, so nice a day to let fools fallow," Bradley replied with a half smile and afterwards didn't stop flaunting his admiration for her. At the end of that evening session they exchanged addresses, phone numbers and e-mails.

Bradley turned to leave, then paused.

"If there is anything I will assure you today, it is that I will get us in Residensea on the fool's day, April first," he said, smiling.

"And me, is that I believe you, Brad," Betsky replied,

all jokes.

Five days later, Betsky received a bouquet of flowers and a ticket for a jaunt on the Residensea.

Surprised, she put a call through to Bradley. "But I was only joking," she said when the phone was picked at the third ring.

"And a joke even more so," replied Bradley. "We will be joining the ship on the early hours of April first," he added.

They joined the ship on a jet that belongs to the tour firm. They landed on the 40,000 gross tons, 644 foot long cruise ship in the early hours of the first of April. It was exactly 4:30 a.m. when the jet touched the floor of the ship's airstrip, having been cleared after ten minutes of hovering over the cruise ship as it coursed its way at 19 knots on the European side of the Atlantic towards the port of Cannes for the annual film festival. The second port the cruise was to call after Rio de Janeiro after three hundred days of cycling the oceans of the universe. At the helipad, they were welcomed by some of the staff members of the ship's 252 staff personnel. The staff crew that welcomed them aboard included a Spaniard, a Frenchman, a Norwegian, and an Italian.

"Bonjone senhores," greeted the Italian who led them aboard the ship while the other staff collected their baggage from the jet. Their documents were checked and they were booked into suite number 518 that measured some 150 square metres, one of the 88 guest suites on the fifth floor of the ship. The ship has about 180 non-guest suites that cost from $2M to $7M and some $200,000 annual maintenance, and measures between 100-300 square metres. It wasn't a bit difficult for them to mingle with the tax dodging resident multi-millionaires and billionaires who have and maintain offices and homes on the cruise ship that circulates the earth. Residents in their 50's and 60's are mostly people who have made their own fortunes. The residents are not residents anywhere and as such are not liable to tax laws of any nation.

Bradley knows a lot about Russia. He is an American and speaks a lot of languages, including Spanish, French, Portuguese, Dutch and Italian, and he plays the piano very well and can quote the Bible from Genesis to Revelations. He quotes lots of human rights and United Nations charters, international laws from international child custody to international tax laws, even interna-

tional arms deals and restrictions and knows the name
of registry and pace by pace court proceedings of the international tribunal for the law of the sea in Hamburg,
Germany, so it was easier for the couple to mix with the
snobbish moneybags who didn't in the least know how
low budget they were.

On their tenth day on the cruise ship, after watching
the movie "Comedy of Time" in the theatre, they went
to the casino where Betsky played the roulette and won
ten stretch bettings, amassing $100,000. Bradley has
never indulged in gambling on the singular reason of
believing that he hasn't got luck in life. He was delighted at the huge amount of money Betsky made within
minutes but he knew very well that one never counts his
riches until he leaves the gambling room. He collected
$50,000 worth of chips, changed them to money, and
walked into the jewellery shop and bought a pair of blue
diamond rings of Lesotho origin. When he went back to
the gambling room, at the table where Betsky was stak-
ing, she was playing her penultimate game. The chips
on her side had diminished. He walked up to her and
reached her ears,

"It's alright now, stop playing," he whispered.

Betsky looked up at him. The urge to go on playing was throbbing inside her but she had only known this gentleman recently and it wouldn't pay to be obstinate with him this early, so she obliged and called off the next game.

As they crossed the doorway of the casino into the wide long corridor, Bradley held Betsky on both shoulders and turned her round to face him. He dropped his voice into a whisper, his eyes fixed on hers.

"Tell me, will you marry me?" he asked.

Betsky's heart skipped in joy as the clause "you marry me, marry me, marry . . ." reverberated in her ears.

"I will marry you now, anytime, any day, anywhere," she replied, crushing him to her.

They stood clasped to each other for some minutes. Betsky looked up at him through a mist of tears and kissed him fiercely on his lips. They went to the shopping mall on the second floor of the ship using the elevator and bought a wedding gown and a black three-piece suit for Bradley. As they waited for the elevator car to descend, a cruise cop appeared at the end of the corridor walking towards them.

"Where is the church, please?" asked Bradley as the

cop walked past them, beaming in greeting.

"Fourth deck, sir," replied the cop, standing erect, his both arms pressed to his sides.

They took the elevator car to the fourth deck. A Catholic priest who introduced himself as Pastor Boyle was present in the church. He wedded them on request and they paid the $200 marriage fee — Residensea's price. Two photographers snapped their photos and resold them to them afterwards.

Ever since then, Bradley had been a doting and adequate husband and Betsky had never heard nor seen him involve in any shady activity. He'd always been dedicated to his research works.

They came back to London after two weeks on Residensea to join Europe in its summer razzle as the awakening sign of summer dawned. Bradley was £20,000 poorer.

Betsky looked at the ring on her ring finger and remember the goose pimples that showered over her that day on seeing the quality of the ring, her most valued single possession before she left for Moscow some three months and two weeks ago on a save-his-soul mission. Bradley had given her a $60,000 emerald necklace on her return from Moscow, yet another demonstration of his interest in material quality. She looked at Bradley in his sleep.

"He only loves good things and grandeur, just like any true American, loud and showy. He is no Mafia, not any bit, still the Brad I know very well," she thought and crawled quietly back into bed and lay beside him. She waited until he woke up and they had breakfast together. It was a typical English breakfast, the bacon was good and the tea tasted great.

"Honey, will you continue short selling stocks or will you devote your total time to research works as before?" asked Betsky, breaking the silence of the breakfast.

Bradley saw the distant fear in her eyes. He knows she isn't a fool, she must've noted the brand of people in the party and must've been trying to put twos together. She hates violence and dangerous association. He understands her, who wouldn't be? Johnny Bandit and his stock of friends and acquaintances in the party ain't a bunch one can easily overlook. Though there were some important people in the society and politicians in the party.

"I've always been a researcher and I will continue

being one but like I told you, the spread of the short sell is large. I want to go into fish farming," replied Bradley.

"What species of fish do you want to rear?" asked Betsky.

"Predatory fishes, sharks, sword fishes, sturgeons principally and then cord fish and other smaller fishes to feed them. The shark and sword fishes flesh will be supplied to eateries and I will use some of the shark cartilages for private research to see if it is actually true that sharks don't suffer cancer as alleged, which gives credence to its massacre and the use of its cartilages for making cancer drugs.

"Some years ago a side result of an experiment I conducted suggested that sharks could get cancer, yes, including cancer of the cartilages," said Bradley.

"Where will you locate the farm?" asked Betsky.

"Somewhere north of England. I've discussed the plans with one farmer who is giving his farm up for sale and going into retirement due to old age and serious illness. It is a four hundred meter square farm compound in excellent condition. The fishes are healthy and the ponds are deep. I only have to introduce Swordfish of the xiphiidea family, and more squids on which they staply feed. Then I will reshuffle the management and it is ready. The financial settlement and the transfer of ownership will be by next week. And before long, we will be supplying the string of top eateries, new ones, and the ones the farm have been supplying in and around UK. I will extend into other European cities and beyond. I'm glad it's not beef so there will be no protectionist restriction in the guise of necessary measures to ensure food safety and shore-off mad cow disease— BSE whose incubation is yet uncertain. I'm very optimistic, it will all work out fine."

"I hope so too, Brad," Betsky said.

"Will we be moving over to north England?" asked Betsky.

Bradley looked at her, paused and squinted in thought.

"I've not thought of that, but, ehmm. . ."

"Then put it into consideration now, 'cause it is equally important," Betsky said.

"I think it wouldn't be necessary to move over there. I will work on the farm only twice a week. I will go from home here in London. I love living in London," said

Bradley.

Betsky looked at him, unaware of his contingency arrangement. She silently wished him well.

They left the Sheraton Hotel for their house a little before midday.

CHAPTER 34

It's been three weeks Tom was waiting for a session with his friend Max. Max's secretary had promised that Max would see him within the month.

Tom wasn't sure how Max made his millions but he knew that Max had been to all the warring African zones and has trusted friends in the Cali village of Colombia, and also meddles in arms and diamond business. All these are well told in Max's financial disposition. It is very obvious that he made a meal of those connections.

Tom knew that Max is in the usury business and people in his, Tom's, situation are the prime clients of the usurers, clients that are often talked into having their debts and businesses financed with loans saddled with excessive interests and fees that are often impossible to honour. Tom doesn't want to negotiate with Max's portfolio managers, 'cause managers often stick to official signing of verbiage documents and forever stick to the sacred rule of money lending – 'what goes out must come back'. Tom wants a personal loan payable when he could, a kind of help.

Tom checked the time, it was 3:30 p.m. and he had no agenda for the rest of the day. He started to get up from the sofa as the phone thrilled on the table. He reached and picked up the receiver.

Rose, Max's secretary was on the line to tell him that Max would want to see him the next morning at 11:30 a.m.

Tom arrived at the office in Oxford Street at 11:20 a.m. and waited another ten minutes before he was ushered into the large airy office by the secretary. Engineer Max, upbeat as usual, was seated behind a large brown oak table at the far end of the opulent office. He was exuding warranted confidence, wearing an excellently tailored suit and diamond cufflinks. He watched as Tom walked across the office towards him, his serious face loosening into a gentle smile as Tom approached. He got up and walked round the table towards Tom and embraced him.

"It's been a long time, Tom," he said.

"Very long indeed, Max," replied Tom.

To Tom, Max was sill the same affable piece. The only difference was that he weighs about ten kilograms more and instead of smoking a stick of silk cut cigarette, he now smokes a pipe of aromatic tobacco sending a white plume of smoke threading up into the lofty office ceiling, and the obvious glow of good living that enveloped him. The office was quite graceful, the gold gilded oak table and oak wooded floor added to the welcoming tranquil atmosphere. Max showed Tom to a seat about five metres from his table and took another seat beside him.

"So Tom Tobby, what spanked you to my office?" Max began. "And what have you been doing all these years?" he added.

Tom looked up at him and remembered that this is a guy he played soccer with, accosted girls and played hide and seek with, as a toddler and teenager, his restrictions and inhibitions fell away. He told Max of his saga with the Soystrol Company and his jail time escapade.

"And for the last few years I've been making my living, moderate though, moving in and out of stocks, buying and selling IPO's, renting stocks and returning them to the market after hours and atimes days."

"Do you know much about the swings of the stock market games?" Max chipped in. "I'm not a novice myself though but it is my portfolio and fund managers that do the actual calculations and manipulations. I've been once told that being a novice is more of a challenge than a hindrance and that some investors prefer to jump in and swim, learning and discovering new rules along the way."

"Well, I attended a day trading training, but the most important thing in trading stocks is to know the fundamental principles, like when interest rates go up stocks go down, and to know which stocks to avoid and why. In an environment where the interest rate is rising, usually cyclical stocks and technology company stocks, which are often valued not for their present earnings but by the profit it is expected to generate in the future, depreciate," Tom said and paused.

"Was it good, your adventure in stock trading?" asked Max.

"It went smoothly fine for some time until I decided to buy and hold an entertainment stock, that's when I crashed, 'cause the stock had an overnight nosedive wiping me out and plunging me into deep choking debt and that's why I came to . . ." said Tom, and swallowed hard.

"I came to your office to ask for help so that I can help myself," he completed, his voice quivering.

"How do you think I can help you?" asked Max placidly.

"I need a bridging loan of £2 M to tide me over," Tom said.

"And how long will you take to pay me back?" asked Max.

"One year," replied Tom.

"Sure?"

"I promise," replied Tom.

"I promise," Max. echoed. The phrase 'I promise' is a borrower's phrase. The phrase makes him remember his past. He had said the same phrase to the late Jonas Savimbi, head of the UNITA rebels in Angola, when he was trying to catch a niche at the UNITA rebels controlled Catoca Diamond mines. It was in Andulo, the

UNITA headquarters in the central highlands of Angola one sunny afternoon. Mr. Jonas Savimbi was sitting behind the large metal table with the UNITA emblem emblazoned on it. Sacks and small bags of diamonds were heaped at one edge of the office room. The UNITA rebels needed weapons in exchange for their diamonds but Max had no weapons up front. He wanted their diamonds up front to buy the western arms and supply to them.

"You can't wage war without money, yes diamonds is money but the currency you most need now to win the war is arms – guns, bombs and fighters, and I can get them for you, the most sophisticated types," Max urged Savimbi.

"Well, thanks for the truism but I need the weapons up-front, all for immediate exchange with the diamonds," Jonas Savimbi had insisted. "If we give you the stones up front, what guarantees do we have for receiving the weapons, that you won't default?" asked Jonas Savimbi.

Max looked him in the eyes, those burrowing sad black eyes.

"My words, I promise." Max said

"Promises are not enough, deeds are," replied Savimbi.

Max then knew that the warmonger wouldn't give him the break he most needed but he tried to press harder.

"I will get back to you with the weapons . . ." he pleaded.

"No way, my young man, no weapons, no diamonds, no deal," Jonas Savimbi said, sitting up and shaking his head side to side in refusal. "Come back here any day with your supply and the diamonds are yours," he added, gesturing towards the heap of glittering stones of diamonds in small brown sack cloth bags at the edge of the room.

"I must see other visitors," he said in a dismissive voice.

Max got to his feet and took his outstretched hand in a firm handshake. He left the office disappointed.

Two months later he was in the Carli village of Columbia where he received the break he needed. The friends in Carli helped him to generous tons of South American white gold, cocaine. Johnny Bandit and the Mob helped in turning the white powder into raw British pounds.

Max was happy and the Mob joyful. It was three months when Max went back to the Andulo highlands of Angola with a fairly large supply of arms. A party was thrown for Max in the UNITA guesthouse. New offensives were launched against the Angolan government forces, who were already closing in to seize the Catoca mine. UNITA had never had a better client. Max left Andulo with bags of diamonds and came back to Andulo only four months later and there it goes.

As Max ruminated on the past, he remembered big-headed, malnourished children scrambling for food in the dustbin of affluent quarters of Luanda, and some elegantly suited western businessmen with smart briefcases stashed with brilliant glittering stones and cargo planes loaded with arms flying across Angolan skies into the rebel's depots.

Max breathed deeply in and looked sidelong at Tom. He knew that Jonas Savimbi didn't give him the break, the trust he needed then because he never knew him from Adam except for the formal introduction they had when he entered the office, but Tom Tobby, he, Max, knows very well. Tom is articulate, careful, and hard working. He takes on his responsibilities and is very dependable. He'd played with Tom as a toddler and teenager when none of them knew who would eventually become rich or poor.

"I won't stiff him," he reached in thought and looked Tom in the face.

"I commiserate with you on your misfortune. We all make mistakes and we all pay for our mistakes but mistakes mustn't be always, so be more careful the next time when you choose and pick your stocks," said Max.

A pause.

"I will give you £2m and you pay me back after twelve months, right?" said Max.

Tom nodded his yes with an almost inaudible "right".

Max got up from his seat and walked to his table. Behind the large oak table he pulled the drawer and scrambled for something and pushed the drawer close.

Tom wondered how many scandalous documents and objects were locked up in the drawer.

Max walked over to the computer and, sitting before it, he punched on the keys to reach his bank.

"What is your bank account number and what bank is it?" he asked Tom.

"Barclay's Bank," replied Tom.

From where Tom was sitting, he could see and read the screen of the computer. He watched Max perk repeatedly on the zero key of the computer keyboard, sixth and then the seventh time, making the figure twenty million instead of two million. Max perked in Tom's account number and bank and waited. Tom saw the cursor move and words scrolled down the screen and the cursor flashing beside the line of words.

Max punched in some numbers with his index fingers, arranging the personalized digital codes that forms his digital signature, completing the transaction and waited for confirmation.

A few words scrolled down the screen and the cursor blinked beside the row: Max pressed the "Y", "E", and "S" keys and then the "Enter" key to accept the transaction. The transaction was approved and confirmed.

"Ready," Max said as he moved towards Tom, "you can withdraw the money from your account," he added.

"Thanks a million times, Max," said Tom.

"Drop in any day for tea," said Max.

Tom got to his feet and took Max's outstretched

hand.

"I'm grateful," he said.

Max walked him to the office door. Tom crossed the doorway into secretary Rose's office and bid her good-bye and made for the elevator in the corridor. His mind was in a complete whirl as he waited for the elevator. The elevator car came and he walked in and descended to the garage to his car and was on his way home.

£20 M was not the script he had in mind before going to Max's office. Was it a piece of luck or temptation? What was he going to do? Go back and tell Max he made a mistake?

"I'd rather you don't," came a still small subconscious voice. "Remember, you'd trusted him when you were youths. You left Alice with him and he betrayed you, slept with her, deflowering her.

" 'You will pay for it in the fullness of time' you'd told him. I'm sure you've not forgiven him or do you hope on another chance? I'd rather you pick this chance. £20 M is good enough a payment for deflowering one's wife," said a mind.

The idea of keeping the £20 M was thrilling though frightening, 'cause he knows Max will discover the slip by Monday before he, Tom, cashes the money, and he will be mad at him.

"But you can stop him from noticing it before Monday. Today is Friday, you have a whopping 72 hours to do it," suggested the mind.

"What?"

"If he's dead before Monday, he won't have time to notice his error and nobody will and you don't owe him, there is no written and signed agreement," said the mind.

Tom paused. The idea was frightening but feasible. If ever, he wouldn't do it himself and he must be very careful in executing the plot. Murder in England carries a sentence of life behind bars.

His heartbeat increased as he thought of life in jail. Thoughts tumbled inside him and five hours later, how to do it best became the question and not the morality of it or the penalty if it went wrong.

He browsed the pages of his diary. Clifford had given him his address and phone number the last time they met. He'd been released from jail after 15 years for planting and setting off a bomb in a government establishment on the mainland London, wounding several people, killing three people, and damaging properties worth hundreds of millions of pounds. He found the number and made for the phone, and dialled the numbers and waited. The phone was answered before the first ring.

"Hey!" came the anxious voice.

"This is Tom," said Tom in reply.

He heard a slight sigh of disappointment at the other end of the line.

"You are waiting for a call, eh?" Tom asked.

"Yes, but not this," said Cliff.

"Don't worry, Cliff, this call is equally important, I bet you. I want to see you, Cliff," said Tom.

"When?" asked Cliff.

"Now."

"No, later in the evening," replied Cliff.

"Now, Cliff, it is urgent, please," Tom urged.

"Very urgent," he added.

"Alright, I will see you. Where?" said Cliff.

"In my house," replied Tom.

Thirty minutes later, Tom peeped through the louver of the blind in his living room to a hoot outside. The taxi was reversing.

Clifford walked towards the front door of the house. Tom went to the door and held it open for Cliff and he entered and Tom closed the door.

"It shows you've been working really very hard since you left the prison," added Cliff.

"Thanks, Cliff," replied Tom.

"Have your seat," he added, gesturing to a single seater cushion.

Cliff sat gently into the seat and crossed his legs.

"Brandy on the rocks?" asked Tom.

"Oh! That's my favourite," said Cliff.

"You once told me," said Tom and walked over to the bar and mixed them two glasses of drinks. He handed Cliff one glass and sipped his as he sat cross-legged on the cushion. He waited until Cliff had the fourth sip of his brandy.

"Cliff," he began, "I have a game and I feel you've a befitting part to play in it."

Clifford listened in silence, propping his head on his right hand placed under his chin as Tom counted out the details of what he called a "befitting" part for him.

"Just enough to explode and kill any living thing in

a 3o meters square office?" asked Cliff when Tom finished.

"Right," Tom replied.

"To whom do I address and mail it?" quizzed Cliff.

"That is outside your part, not even I know. That part has been allocated to the appropriate quarters," replied Tom.

"Not difficult," said Cliff. "But I need time to think about it."

"Not much time is left, Cliff, we want it ready before Sunday morning," said Tom.

"I will give you a ring," said Cliff. He finished his drink in one draught and upped to leave.

Tom called a taxi for him. The cab arrived five minutes later and hooted. Tom escorted him to the cab.

"I'm waiting for your call, Cliff," said Tom as he closed the back door of the black cab.

It was only four months that Clifford, an ex-IRA guerrilla, had been on the streets of England a free man. To Cliff, so much had changed and so much had also remained the same. It is spring and Dalies Diana flowers are blossoming in English front gardens and Londoners are full of joy of the spring. The British pounds have not sunk in isolation from the Euro, the European nascent common currency, as predicted by the sceptics. Greenwich Village had been domed with the world's largest domed structure and the Jubilee line has been completed. River Thames has been purified to crystal clarity and now harbours salmon and 81 species of other fishes after over 150 years of absence. Royal crests have been recalled from establishments as plutocrats are weakened by deaths and fallout of favour with Buckingham Palace, and the Tesco supermarket has been ordained. The 1500 annual Christmas pudding purchase for the Royal family staff members have been signed to Tesco supermarket. With the help of the Yankees, peace has been achieved in Northern Ireland and the IRA have surrendered and disarmed and a splinter group, the continuity IRA, is operating, though Cliff doesn't like their principles. The power sharing government in Belfast has taken shape. And according to the scientists in the University of New South Wales in Sydney, Australia, bubbles in a glass of Guinness Stout now travel downwards instead of upwards, thus defying the laws of nature, beneficial though according to the researchers, but . . .

Times are really changing and the wind of change is gathering momentum but in Clifford is still the same man and spirit that made and exploded bombs some fifteen years back, targeting mainland government property and personnel. Clifford still had the letter bomb making facilities at the tips of his fingers. It isn't a bad offer that Tom has given him, not just for the generous price, £100,000. Though he knows that maintaining life now is going to be difficult, as he is sure he won't find a job 'cause his genetic information as required by employers will reveal his violent nature and the diabetic history of his family, but mainly because making and setting off bombs on the mainland UK, be it on individual interests or on government property, is part of not accepting and swearing allegiance to the mainland crown, and he is forever bent on not swearing allegiance to the mainland crown that held him a prisoner for a decade and a half.

"Agreed," mumbled Cliff to himself.

Tom had said it is urgent and must be ready by Sunday morning, so if he must do it, he must start now.

He reached the phone and dialled Tom's number. Tom picked the phone at the first ring.

"We have a deal," Cliff said into the mouthpiece without preamble.

"Tom?" he added.

"Yes, a deal?" replied Tom.

"Yes, Cliff confirmed. "It will be ready by tomorrow night," he added.

"Very good," said Tom.

"Until tomorrow," said Cliff and hung.

It was 11:30 p.m. Saturday night when Cliff delivered the letter to Tom in his house.

"Built to precision, just as you recommended, could wipe out any living thing within a 30 meters square radius on the explosion," said Cliff.

He left with the same cab that brought him.

Tom dropped the letter into the post the next morning.

Rose, Max's secretary picked the letter from the office mailbox on Monday morning and put it in the silver salver amongst other letters for Max.

Max arrived at the office at 10:00 a.m. as usual and walked straight to his table. He checked his electronic mail and reached for the letters in the salver. He picked the first letter and ripped it open with the gold letter opener. A pleasant smile suffused his face as he read. Mary, his girlfriend, penned her love for him. He put the letter aside and picked the next one. He slipped the gold letter opener under the flap of the envelop and pulled.

Boom! Boooom!! and Boooommmm! Came the explosion.

Rose dived under her table out of fear from the enormous deafening banging noise. The building vibrated. The force of the explosion threw Max from his seat up into the air, smashing him through the wide glass windowpane that offers a panoramic view of the street below, and threw him down the seventy meters height of his office floor and smashed him onto the street below, killing him instantly.

The evening tabloids had it that Max died from a letter bomb explosion. The last big business he transacted was a transfer of £20M into one Mr. Tom Tobby's account. "Gift or debt? Nobody knows", wrote the tabloids.

Rose didn't remember the name of the sender. She was only sure that it wasn't a familiar name or a regular correspondent of Max's. This made the Scotland Yard investigation nipped in the bud 'cause there was no lead clue. Scotland Yard only confirmed that the bomb was homemade.

For routine questioning, Scotland Yard questioned Tom and released him. Tom is now a millionaire — a lifelong dream come true.

Tom had never felt more capacitated in life than now, a warranted capacitation, £20m is not £20 hundred. It can capacitate anyone but Tom knew that it doesn't end at being a millionaire, laying his palm on a few tens of millions. He knew that if he must remain a millionaire and ultimately a multi-millionaire that he must rightly invest this fortune he robbed from Max.

"No, acquired," he corrected in thought.

He must act and think like a millionaire to remain a millionaire and above all must invest like a millionaire. He's put some of the money in his brokerage account to meet margin calls and loans and save his house from creditors. Before buying the shares of the Layne Heller Ltd., the medical stent makers that have recently announced they will insert their new product on a patient's coronary artery, and that the patient is Bob Joey, Europe's most popular pop star. Tom knew that if the surgery becomes successful then the stock prices of the device and company would rise sharply but if it became a failure, yet another risk. But Bob Joey the pop star is so rich and popular that researchers, inventors, promoters and the doctors working with the stent must be sure and careful before using him as the first person to test the experimental device. Tom, a prudent investor, checked the list of shareholders of the stent company. Dr. Claim who was the lead surgeon of the operation, the nurses and all the surgery crew, the promoters and inventors of the device are all shareholders of the company. The surgery crew would not only earn kudos for a successful surgery but also would earn enormous wealth for a positive result. Tom was impressed and sure of the stock, and he made his engress into the stock with £2M increasing the £2b tally of shares traded daily on the London Stock Exchange. Tom was back to trading.

He had wanted to move into biotech stocks but the precipitous movement of the stocks was flashing a warning sign to him. Now a long term investor, he doesn't want to make any mistakes similar to that he made with the entertainment stock that flawed him. Besides, in the biotech sector, Tom believes that manufacturing, discovery and invention is much better than trading its stocks. It has made overnight multi-millionaires out of single digit millionaires.

CHAPTER 35

Thoughts flew down Tom's mind as he sat on the cushion in the living room of his house. He was showered with goose pimples at the thought of Kate and marriage and wondered how other men who are successful with their marriage had managed to handle it. He was sure that he can't manage the complexity of the marriage society any more. He'd rather stay single for the rest of his life.

Mr. Adams suddenly flashed to mind. Tom could see him vividly sticking out his tongue at him in the courtroom before he, Tom, was hurled out of the courtroom into the prison vehicle. He became nervously excited at the thought of Adams.

"Revenge is most flavoured when it is cold and forgotten, they say," he murmured.

But how is he going to avenge Mr. Adams now? At the moment, he has no idea of a befitting 'eye for an eye' revenge. Putting Mr. Adams behind bars for at least eleven months will be good for starters.

"Difficult," he mused. "Not any dirt to beat up against him, at least at this moment," he added.

It was 4:30 p.m. when he logged onto the Internet and navigated through the corporate information site of the Soystrol Company Ltd. Mr. Adams was no longer the manager of the Soystrol Company.

From the corporate information site of the London Stock Exchange, he read the names of corporate managers of companies listed with the LSE and found out that Mr. Adams became the manager of the Strol chain of restaurants, a subsidiary of Soystrol Ltd. Satisfied, he logged off.

"Why was he removed from the Soystrol general management to a subsidiary company?" he thought. "This might be the key to the dirt I most need about him."

Though Gladys, the Soystrol Company secretary, still works with the Soystrol Company, Tom couldn't be sure she still lives in her home in Hammersmith. He wouldn't want to meet her anywhere near the Soystrol establishment lest people see them together and report to the management. Tom went into his room and tarted up himself and was on his way to Gladys' house in Hammersmith. The traffic was thin and he was there on time.

It was a twenty-minute drive from his house to Hammersmith. He stopped and parked at the head of the road, turned into her street and waited inside the car. Another twenty minutes crawled by before, he saw from the side mirror, Gladys' car approached. He got out and waved her down as she turned into the street. Gladys moved about fifty meters before stopping. Tom could see as she peered into her car's side mirror to catch a view of him as he approached on foot. He walked to the passenger's left side of the car and crouched over the glass window of the passenger's front door.

"Oh, Tom," Gladys called out. "You?" she added, surprised.

Surprise was the only registered emotion on her face. If there was any other emotion she felt, she didn't let it show.

"Yes, it's me," Tom replied.

"Get in," said Gladys, stretching to open the door for him.

Tom got in the front passenger's seat.

"What are you doing here?" asked Gladys, as Tom adjusted himself in the seat.

"I'm going somewhere in this neighbourhood. I overtook you on the freeway but you didn't notice me, so I decided to stop and say hello to you. It's been a long time. So how are you?" said Tom.

"So-so, Tom," said Gladys.

"They defeated you in the court. I heard your lawyer wasn't that good. When did you come out from the prison?" asked Gladys.

"It's been long. I stayed eleven months and was granted a prime ministerial pardon.

"What of Mr. Adams?" Tom asked.

"Mr. Adams is no longer with us, he's now with the Strol Restaurants as their manager," replied Gladys.

"Why? Promotion?" Tom probed, happy that she at least gave the info freely without hemming and ehm-ming.

"It's demotion rather. Mr. Adams encouraged the

planting of genetically modified seeds of soybean on the Soystrol farmland, the most abhorred type of bio-tech seeds, those genetically modified to produce their own pesticides. And as you know the farmland is leased from the Church of England whose ethical investment advisory group recommended that church lands not be used to grow biotech crops because of the uncertainty over their safety. So he was removed from the general management and put where he will have less access to general decisions. He's doing fine there. The last time we spoke, he said he was happy there. And you? How has it been? Rough, eh? Got a new job?" asked Gladys.

"Not yet," Tom said.

"But it's alright with me. I'm fine and healthy," he added quickly.

"I must hurry Gladys, I will call you some other day," said Tom.

"It's okay Tom, drop in any day for tea," replied Gladys.

Tom opened the car door and stepped into the street and walked to his car at the head of the street.

The information he got was not enough dirt to scratch Mr. Adams, but it's information nonetheless. Mr. Adams has had a problem with the management of the Soystrol Company and if anything else happens to the management of the Strol chain of restaurants, he will once again be relegated or resigned. Tom knew the Strol restaurants, it's a big and popular chain of restaurants, all its branches are visited by the high and the mighty, monied businessmen, ambassadors, stars, and politicians, but Tom had never dined or lunched there. There are about four branches of the restaurant in the city of London alone to serve the brutal size of the city and its vast moneyed class, and two in Manchester city.

Five days later, at 12:00 noon, Tom was at the Fulham branch of the Strol restaurant. The number of clients in the restaurant wasn't that high. He left the restaurant after eating a light meal and paying a bill of £300. At 2:30 p.m. he was at the Oxford Street branch of the restaurant. The décor was samey with that of the Fulham branch, a traditional décor of large tables, mirrors, oil portraits, and large expensive antique wall clock, and the beaming dark suited waiters. Tom chose a non-reserved table at the end of the hall. He read the menu as the waiter waited beside. He finally called out his order and the waiter penned them down. He was served hors d'oeuvres, specially prepared caviar followed by a smoked chunk of shark flesh with béarnaise potatoes, a fair dose of paprika and green vegetables, and wild mushrooms, a bottle of Larose St. Julien – a red Bordeaux wine. Dessert was finely chopped mixture of tropical fruits. He enjoyed his meal immensely. On his way home, Tom pondered on what to do to bring problems to the Strol chain of restaurants, to dislodge Mr. Adams from its alpine manager's seat.

If E. coli 0157 strains and or salmonella were to be sprayed on the green vegetables, the chopped fruit dessert or the mushrooms, diarrhea would terrorize the Strol restaurant priggish clients, and Adams would be obviously affected, but this plan would involve finding out who the Strol restaurant greengrocers and fruiterers are, and then through them poison the Strol restaurant dishes, or through their chefs, but it would be involving a whole lot of people thus making himself, Tom, and the most needed secrecy of the plot vulnerable to being easily unmasked by the investigators. And if he is ever linked again and charged for food poisoning and disrupting public health, found guilty and hurled to jail again, he was sure he won't be able to stand it for the second time. He dispensed the idea based on this, and besides, how would the expenses be recovered? Tom had learnt the principle of money management – 'what goes out must come back in', be it for entertainment, pleasure or revenge. He knew that the Strol restaurant warrants are listed on the London Stock Exchange. Warrants cost a fraction of the cost of the stock. The Strol stock is going for £100 per share.

Thoughts and thoughts tumbled down Tom's mind; using Cliff once again, Cliff, now a very trusted ally. He would spend just a fraction of the Strol stock price to cause a hell of a headache to Mr. Adams whom he knew very well would resign to take the blame for the security lapse in the Strol restaurant chain.

This time, Cliff will get more clearly involved than before, but there is no problem, he is assured, because Cliff is an old soldier, and with old soldiers things hardly ever go wrong.

The idea was as exciting to him as the first time he had sex and the ease with which the idea flowed down his mind made it even more seemingly feasible.

The next day Tom bought the put warrant of the Strol restaurant stock. The writer of the put warrant, Lloyds

Bank, who were also the Strol restaurant bankers, wrote the option on behalf of the Strol chain of restaurants. The £70 put warrant was traded at £3. Tom bought one million warrant shares at £3m. The writer, seller never believed that the stock would fall to such a low price between July and the fourth of January the following year, it is a bullish period for restaurant stocks. If the share price falls below £70 to worthless, as Tom was plotting, Tom would earn £67 per option because the seller who was paid £3 was required to deliver a share for £70, so for the possibility of earning £3, the seller would have to lose £67 per share and Tom by risking £3 per share would get £67 payoff. Tom was sure that his plot, with the help from Cliff, could not go wrong.

CHAPTER 36

Bradley has stopped the weekly addition of excess mercury to the ponds and the farms in north England had been supplying eateries, including the Strol chain of restaurants. The epidemic of mercury poisoning was evident from the number of patients in the hospitals and people with early symptoms in the streets.

Bradley had just discovered that he misrepresented the chemical composition of the compound found in the gut of the Juba frog. One component was missing in his diary: the chemical for making the drug that will help the natural production of the essential enzyme that could cure the orphan disease and its symptoms as is found in mercury poisoning – shaking, low coordination, stumbling and low reflexes. The chemical and even the enzyme couldn't be artificially synthesized without a natural substrate as he'd envisioned earlier.

He'd thought of the horn of Africa – Ethiopia, the Juba forest and shrine of Ethiopia and the thatched huts of the villages. The whole lot of the European population was in danger and Bradley was profoundly concerned. He caused it with the sole intention of solving it, and putting the drug on the shelves of all the pharmacy round the globe.

Lazarus, the Ethiopian villager, must've been dead by now, considering the life span of an average African and his age then in the 50's, the Ethiopian famine not far from his mind and the rest of the villagers and Lazarus' children and kin must've known how much he, Bradley, and company callously defaulted on their promise. And only the Juba frogs of the shrine, the chemical in its guts, can save the English and the western population.

CHAPTER 37
London Hilton Hotel
June 1999

Gabriel was waiting at the front door of Tom's house when Tom got home. Tom was rather happy on seeing him, he'd received his letter weeks ago, where Gabriel wrote of his coming release from the prison and Tom had replied, offering to harbour him in his house.

They embraced and shook hands. It had only been few years that they had not seen each other, but it seemed an eternity. Tom opened the front door and they got into the house. Tom showed him around the house and Gabriel was really impressed at the relative grandeur of Tom's house. Tom later ran the bath for him, and Gabriel had his bath and joined him in the sitting room.

"Could you believe that I'm totally free of the parasitic HIV virus? The last test I had three weeks before my release showed that not a single virus is left in my bloodstream. God is great, Tom," Gabriel said happily.

"Faith is a wonderful thing," Tom said, pondering whether to tell him what he did in the prison blood bank. He decided against it.

"It's better to leave him with his faith, besides if a test result some three weeks back showed no HIV virus in his system, then he's free of the virus," Tom thought.

"Congratulations!" said Tom. "You can survive anything and anywhere now. You survived prison and the HIV virus, you can survive hell, you're a strong guy."

"Thanks, Tom," replied Gabriel.

"And thank you too for providing the opportunity for us to help ourselves," mumbled Tom, a notch short of audibility.

"Eh?" inquired Gabriel.

"No, nothing," replied Tom.

A pause.

"Tom, I want a glass of cold beer," said Gabriel.

"There is some beer in the fridge," Tom said, and

started to get up to fetch a can of beer for him.

"No, Tom, I want a glass of draught beer in an open place, I mean a pub," said Gabriel.

"In a pub? That's good, let's go and celebrate your release from prison, your freedom," said Tom, adding quickly, "and in a very good pub!"

Tom went into the room and threw a shirt on. They drove to the Hilton Hotels Limited and selected a table in the centre of the lounge bar and ordered beer, draught beer.

Bradley was seated at a table at the end of the lounge bar, taking solace in drinking amidst ruminations on how to help the European and English public health. He looked across the faces of the people in the lounge, some faces that had stayed long in the bar were already drooping from drunkenness, others excited, and the new arrivals were still sober, but there was something familiar about the sober young black man sitting quietly with his company in the centre of the lounge.

Watching him smoke and sip his drink, it dawned on Bradley that the fresh-faced happy looking black man was the same that saved their lives from the soldiers of the Juba god, the same man that showed them the house of the Juba shrine priest and later led them back to the Juba forest shrine in defiance of the priest's decision, and helped them with a good measure of bio-samples. The man, Lazarus...they'd promised so much to him, but never returned to compensate and fulfill their promise. The man in the fifties, the Ethiopian, he had remembered some days ago when he discovered that the synthetic version, without a natural substrate, of the chemical found in the gut of the Juba frog is not feasible for making the drug most needed to help the public health. The public health he deliberately and single-handedly infested.

Looking at the young man in the centre of the bar, Bradley could remember quite vividly as they walked down the lonely narrow dirty path that separated the village from the shrine as they re-entered the shrine, the two monkeys standing on their hind legs with quizzical squints in their eyes, their forelegs resting on a branch of a shrub, the lions, their mouths curved back and up in a halted growl. He remembered the snakes, tigers and wolves, staring with dilated eyes, all in an anxious mood as they moved towards the black rock, fringed by lush greenery from where crystal clear water tumbles out forming the brook that rumbles on its serpentine course down the bush into the forest beyond. The hyenas that crossed the brook and turned into the greenery that fringed the black rock, and the strange quietness that descended over the environment as the creature walked into the rock and the trance-like sensation he and his colleagues felt at the time while Lazarus called out greetings, appeals and praises to the creature, as Lazarus bowed three times and ordered them to do the same and they obliged.

"We can collect any sample we need now," Lazarus had told them at the end of it all.

Gabriel took another draught from his goblet as Bradley wrestled with the past. Bradley wiped his left hand across his face, as if to wipe out sleepiness, but it wasn't surrealism, it was retrospect. He coughed out loud to make sure he was still conscious and heads turned towards him. The man in the centre of his gaze had not added any sign of aging to what he looked like in the fifties. Bradley knew much about cryogenics. Cryonics is the deep-freezing at death of human bodies for preservation and possible revival in the future.

Cryonics is the only known scientific magic that

could shield Lazarus this much, and so perfectly, from the ravages of time, but so far nobody had been unfrozen and brought back to life by cryonics.

Gabriel suddenly looked Bradley's way and their gaze locked for a second. Gabriel smiled, a polite smile, and looked away. No shadow of doubt was left in Bradley. The man was Lazarus or at least his reincarnate.

Bradley got to his feet and walked over to their table.

"Excuse me, gentlemen, may I share the table with you?" asked Bradley.

Gabriel and Tom exchanged glances.

"Sure!" said Tom with a half smile.

Gabriel kept mute.

Bradley pulled a chair and sat down.

"I'm Bradley," he said.

"Tom."

"Gabriel."

"You changed your name?" asked Bradley.

"How do you mean?" replied Gabriel.

"I mustn't be mistaking you for one Mr. Lazarus Hailea, an Ethiopian?" quizzed Bradley, looking Gabriel in the eyes.

"Lazarus Hailea?" said Gabriel.

"Yes," said Bradley.

"And you are?" quizzed Gabriel.

"Bradley."

"When and where did you meet and know Mr. Lazarus Hailea?" asked Gabriel.

"In the fifties, in Ethiopia," Bradley said.

"Are you a biotechnologist?"

"Yes I am," replied Bradley.

"I'm not Lazarus Hailea, I'm Gabriel Kicke Hailea. Lazarus is my father," said Gabriel as flashes of memories tumbled down his mind – his father telling him about one Mr. Bradley, the spokesman of the western group of biohunters that promised him and he, Lazarus, in turn promised the Juba god. He had believed in them and believed that one day they would be back. "It might take long though but definitely he will be back to the land of Juba to pay his debt and tribute to the Juba god," his father would say. And today he, Gabriel, is here with Bradley in the flesh and bone in the heart of England.

"What a perfect resemblance," said Bradley.

Gabriel looked slowly away, blinking back tears.

"My father died years ago from the wrath of the Juba god for having defaulted on his promise. You killed my father and destroyed our family, Mr. Bradley," said Gabriel, looking back at Bradley.

"What you and your crew did to my father and my family was a callous display of ingratitude. Daddy died an outcast in his own land and the same was closing in on me before I took an attitude," said Gabriel.

Bradley tried to explain but there wasn't much to explain and defend. He knew much better than to argue. They didn't keep their promise.

"It was wrong of me, morally and otherwise. I wouldn't say legally, because that was before fairness in biodiversity was signed into law," Bradley said, a hangdog expression on his face.

"What are you doing in England?" he asked, trying to change the subject.

Gabriel told him exactly the same thing he'd told Tom Tobby in jail.

"I was released from prison today," he concluded.

Bradley was filled with indignation, then shame. He cupped his hand to his face, shaking his head from side to side.

"Where are you staying now?" he asked, looking up at Gabriel.

"He is staying in my house now, but before long we will find him his own apartment. The estate agent is busy finding him a place," Tom chipped in.

Bradley nodded understandingly.

Silence reigned as Bradley pondered his unusual luck at meeting Gabriel, a possible lead back to the Juba shrine and the Juba frog, the chemical in its gut and the eventual production of the drugs to alleviate the public health. He will first meet his decades-long promise and pay any other promise up front.

Gabriel was studying Bradley, wondering why such a rich, gentle and reasonable looking man could be such a liar, a cheat, who cheated and deceived his poor illiterate father to his death.

And Tom looked Gabriel over.

"Poor Gab," he thought, "always in the use."

He turned to Bradley. "So, you are a biotechnologist?" he asked, breaking the silence.

"Yes I am, and you?" replied Bradley.

"I'm an investor," replied Tom.

"And you are Tom?" said Bradley.

"Tom Tobby, yes," said Tom.

"Oh, Tom Tobby, I've read much about you in the tabloids. You and Max the millionaire," said Bradley.

"Is it?" Tom said.

Gabriel took a long draught of his beer, excused himself and made for the men's room.

"It's really a shame. We collected the bio-samples from the forest shrine in his Juba village and we didn't go back to make burnt offerings to the god of the shrine as we promised. His father helped us immensely. We collected barley samples and frogs. The barley was sent to California where it was crossbred to ward off yellow dwarf virus from farm crops. And today, there is nothing I need more than I need the Juba frog, because of the chemical in its gut to develop a drug for the cure of a disease, a rare orphan disease that is ailing the European public. It is very good that I met him here today," Bradley confessed.

"You are developing a new drug?" asked Tom.

"Yes, all I need now is the Juba frog and more capital for the venture," replied Bradley.

"The capital?" asked Tom.

"Yes, and the capital," said Bradley, laying emphasis

on the 'and'.

Tom saw Gabriel approaching.

"Let's meet, on the twentieth of this month, next week. As for the Juba frog, I will speak with Gabriel."

"Here, in this lounge, 12:00 noon, right?"

"Right," replied Bradley.

Gabriel eased into his seat and crossed his legs.

Tom beckoned a waiter.

"The bill, please," he said when the waiter came.

The waiter hurried away and came back minutes later. Tom gave him a credit card.

"Your pen please," Bradley said to the waiter as he was about to leave.

The man turned and gave him a pen and a piece of paper he pulled from a pad. Bradley penned a few numbers on the paper and gave it to Tom.

"I'm sorry, I've got no cards on me. Give me a call," he said as he handed him the piece of paper. "When will you be going back to Ethiopia?" Bradley said, turning to Gabriel.

"Ehmm, I don't know yet," said Gabriel.

The waiter brought back the credit card and Tom picked it up from the saucer.

"Thank you, sir," said the waiter.

"We must leave now," said Tom, getting to his feet.

"We will see later," Bradley said to Gabriel.

"I hope so," Gabriel replied.

Gabriel and Tom left the lounge bar and drove towards the north. Tom left Gabriel at the estate agent's place north of London.

CHAPTER 38

Clifford arrived two minutes behind schedule but Tom wasn't at the arena. Tom was speeding towards south-east London to meet Cliff at the moment.

He met Cliff at the park twenty minutes later, and they walked up and down as Tom spelt out the plot. Cliff was enchanted with the idea. Every bit of it was enthralling. It triggered the IRA memories in him. He loved it, the adrenaline, the fear and exhaustion on the victims' faces, the thrill of seeing buildings explode and crumble, the search by the rescue crew for survivors and dead bodies, the sight of blood-stained victims, mostly Protestants, being transferred into ambulances. Then the ensuing chase by Scotland Yard for the perpetrators, and the run, the dodge not to be unmasked and face a date in the court. It was enthralling. And Tom would make him relive this experience again.

"Marvellous!" he said.

"They decommissioned the IRA, but me, Cliff Dogood, the old soldier, they can't decommission. They never die, old soldiers," thought Clifford.

Cliff has always believed in and trusted his strength. Strength, he has always believed, is acting on one's beliefs, irrespective of the popular opinion. It is about consistency over time. Now he knows that driving the English out of Northern Ireland has not been the only driving force for setting explosives on the mainland but rather the odium of their encroachment and the rancour it caused among the Irish folk.

He went through the plot by mind as Tom walked silently beside him, waiting for questions. Cliff laughed, he was imagining his friends — Martin, Remmick, Allen and Walter, fisting in an unprovoked fight just to cause confusion and embarrassment to the priggish clients of the Strol restaurant in Manchester and he, Cliff, sneaking in and out of the four branches of the Strol restaurants in the city of London with his bomb laden briefcase.

"What's funny?" asked Tom.

"No, nothing," Cliff replied, adding, "And I must make a good impression of a gentleman to be allowed into the restaurant, eh?"

"Yes, Cliff, you are not any known star and as such a good suit and tie will facilitate entrance. They won't allow you in without a tie. They might provide you with one at the entrance, but don't call any unnecessary attention to yourself. Make no mistakes, and try as much as you can not to speak, your accent Cliff, and lad-di-daing the classic upper class accent will be most betraying. Just be yourself but speak as little as you can," said Tom.

"Ta!" replied Cliff.

* * *

The one bedroom apartment that Gabriel had gone to inspect was clean, the carpets were vacuumed, and the walls were newly painted. Gabriel opened the bedroom window and sat on the bed, and began to ruminate about what Tom had just told him while they were driving to the estate agent's office, about going back to Ethiopia and the Juba shrine frogs. He tried to coin out a balance between his late father's past mistakes, his present status in the Juba village and the future.

"My father was used and cheated, but me?

No!

Once beaten, twice shy, they say. Something must've gone wrong with the samples Bradley and his colleagues collected, otherwise he wouldn't be needing a second batch," thought Gabriel.

"Trust the Juba God," he added out loud.

That's why he must recognize the power and resources he has at hand now, to decide and negotiate. Whatever help they need he will give them but for a price and up front of course. They can't cheat much now, though, not because Bradley wouldn't want to, but because laws have been put in place today against theft of biospecimens to ensure their equitable use. He will negotiate with Bradley, because any benefit, which will be manipulated from it, will be to the service of humanity, just as his father promised the Juba god. But he must be shrewd when he negotiates.

He started towards the front door. He liked the flat.

He moved in two days later.

CHAPTER 39
London, England
July 1999

Tom arrived late at his house. He fed the dog and Eddy, the cat, and chained the dog in the kennel. As always, Eddy the cat was free. Tom has always wished that Kate had taken the cat with her. He doesn't like cats.

He set the alarm clock for seven o'clock and went to bed. It was the nineteenth of July and he had a sound dreamless sleep until he tried to wake and get out of bed the next morning, the twentieth of July.

When he arrived at the lounge bar of the Hilton Hotels at 12:00 noon, Bradley was already waiting, sitting at the same table he and Gabriel had left him a week ago, sipping cold fresh strawberry juice. He smiled and upped when Tom approached the table, and took Tom's outstretched arm in a handshake.

"And Gabriel?" he asked.

"He is fine, I suppose, he parked into an apartment north of London some five days back. It is a nice apartment," replied Tom as he drew a chair to sit down.

Without further preamble, Bradley went on to explain the theme of their meeting.

"Like I told you last week," Bradley started, and Tom listened showing no expression to Bradley's explanation about the chemical in the gut of the Juba shrine frog and how it will help in developing his new drug that enhances the release and provides the optimum condition for the enzyme that cures the orphan disease and mercury poisoning.

Tom understood and enjoyed every bit of the discussion, even at Bradley's insinuation.

". . . not as easy and lucky a strike as outliving a generous creditor," an insinuation he, Tom, somehow provoked. But what really beats is not the insinuation itself but how Bradley came to know about his creditor, Max, not just knowing him but knowing that Max was his creditor. After all, it wasn't written in any of the tabloids that the money transferred into Tom's account by

Max before his death was a loan.

Tom looked up at Bradley and gazed vacantly into his face.

"I like the idea," he said finally, and dropped his gaze and took a quick sip of his tea. "You can count on me. We can go to Ethiopia anytime you are ready. Gabriel has been spoken to," he added, and reached his breast pocket. "Here!" he said, pushing a business card to Bradley.

Bradley picked the card and glanced at it. "I will give you a call," he said, as Tom rose to go. "Extend my greetings to Gabriel," added Bradley

CHAPTER 40

It was 8:00 a.m., trading in the London Stock Exchange has opened and the Strol restaurant stock was appreciating.

Cliff checked the electronics of the explosives. The cloned digits of the wave receptor on each of the three bombs were in order. He wrapped the first sheet of gift papers round the three bombs and then the second sheet and the third. He tied the ribbons round the parcels making a bow knot on each, making the explosive ensembles into attractive parcels. He put the three parcels into his briefcase then removed his hand gloves.

He spent the next hour before a full-length mirror. The bushy eyebrow, the trimmed moustache and the clean shave, the blonde wig and the pair of reading glasses gave him a new and disguised outlook. In his wardrobe he chose the black Armani suit. A lighter colour would have been more suitable to the day's weather, but he was going to blast three of the four branches of the Strol restaurant, and a lot of people would be wounded, others sore frightened, and the most unfortunate few, if any, would die. Black is the colour of death and mourning, a colour of seriousness and there was so much to be serious about that day.

"I will start mourning them before they drop dead, wounded or fainted," he thought as he slipped on the suit. He put on oxblood shoes to match the dark red tie. He selected two other ties, a brown one and a blue tie and put them in the small paper sack containing his disguise kit – an auburn wig, a trimmed teddy bear, a bushy eyebrow and a curly silver sprinkled black wig, and tucked the lot into the briefcase. With the briefcase in hand, he went back to the mirror to look at the ensemble. He adjusted his tie and turned to his left and then to his right. He was most impressed and satisfied with the reflection in the mirror – a gentleman.

His last meeting with Tom came to mind.

"A good suit and tie will do," Tom had told him.

"Now who said I'm not a bigwig?" he murmured sat-isfactorily.

In the garage, he placed the briefcase on the front passenger seat of the Ford Escort and walked round the car to the driver's side and gunned the engine to life. As he drove into the busy street that intersects his street, the MI5 agent who had been assigned to monitor him since his release from jail was reading a newspaper inside his car parked by the shoulder of the street. He peered at him as he drove past; the man be-hind the wheel was not his man but the car was his. He came down the car and watched the car as it drove down the street and pulled off in front of a gallery down the street. Cliff came out of the car and walked into the gal-lery, his briefcase at hand. He crossed the gallery into the street behind and waved down a taxi. He wasn't sure of any trail but it is a routine precaution especially on a hit day as today, so as to live up to the security tact-fulness that committing crimes in the English society with the oldest police force on the planet demands. And for a man marked as a terrorist in Britain who has been 15 years behind bars and whose hostel cellmate in the prison was questioned some months back for a bomb blast. The English police force, he knows, must have dug out all these facts and who knows how many times he's been seen and photographed with Tom. Cliff is quite on track on his security routine. The MI5 agent moved forward and, standing beside the road, he kept watch on the car parked in front of the gallery while the lady in the front passenger seat of his car kept watch on other cars coming into and out of the street where Cliff lives. Another two hours went by before the MI5 agent called their control office to report the situation.

"Fieldman number 10 is speaking," he began saying into his phone.

"His car came out from his house some two hours ago, driven by a blond dark suited man. The car is parked in the front of the gallery down the street next to the street where he resides. The blond man has been inside the gallery since then and till now I have not seen our man," he said.

"Give another thirty minutes and keep watch on the car," said the man at the London central MI5 office.

The taxi dropped Cliff off at Allen's house southeast of London. Allen, in the company of Remmick and Walter, was in Manchester at that moment. A car hired in

Walter's name the day before was parked inside Allen's garage.

Clifford drove away in the hired car. The Fulham branch of the Strol restaurant was the last of the three restaurants he chose to visit after leaving the Chelsea branch. He'd changed into the auburn wig, the teddy bear, without the reading glasses, when he visited the Chelsea branch of the restaurant. He left the Chelsea branch and speeded towards Fulham. Just before engressing the Fulham Palace Road, he pulled onto the road shoulder and wound up the tinted glass window of the Honda Civic car. Using the car's rear-view mirror he removed the auburn wig and put on the silver sprinkled black wig, and the brown tie was replaced with the blue tie, the bushy eyebrow was replaced with a neatly brushed one. And he preferred his clean-shaven face to the trimmed teddy bear and a clean upper lip was preferred to the trimmed moustache. He put the reading glasses back in place. The whole ensemble gave him the look of a university don. He wound down the car window glass and nudged the car into traffic and continued towards Fulham. His phone vibrated with a call as he stepped into the elevator car. He stepped backwards and out of the elevator car, and looked at the caller display panel of the handset but the number on display was not one he was familiar with.

"Who could this be?" he mused as he lifted the phone to his right ear.

"Hello?" he said softly into the mouthpiece.

"Where are you, John?" came a lady's voice.

"Who is this?" he asked.

"Helen," said the lady, adding, "but baby don't tell me you don't recognize my voice."

"I'm afraid you've got a wrong number, Helen," Cliff said.

"Wrong number?" said the lady, sounding surprised. "Isn't this 723. . ." she asked.

"No," interrupted Cliff, not allowing her to finish.

"Sorry," she said and hung up.

The lady came out of the phone booth and crossed the street to their car.

"Got him?" asked the MI5 agent.

"Yes," she said.

He put a call from his cellular phone through to the office.

"This is field man ten, we've spoken with him just

now," he said into the phone.

"Yeah! We've got the antenna with which the call was transmitted to him and within minutes we will have the cellular antenna with which he received your call and we will give you his location. Right?"

"OK!" replied field man ten and hung.

Clifford walked back into the elevator and ascended to the fourth floor of the building, to the restaurant. He looked around to see the position of the camera as the waiter approached him, but the camera wasn't anywhere in plain view.

He walked to the far end of the restaurant and chose a table. He placed his order and waited.

He looked around the restaurant. The waiters were busy and none of the clients were looking his way. He opened his briefcase and, using the flap of the briefcase, he shielded his hand and face from the view of anyone. He placed the white silk handkerchief over the parcel and brought it out and slipped it into the flowerpot beside his table. The lush broad green weeping leaves of the flower plant covered the parcel from view. He put the handkerchief back into the briefcase and closed it. He looked across the faces of the clients in the restaurant as they munched on their meal and wondered who among them would survive the bomb blast and who was having their last lunch. The waiter came forward pushing the lunch wagon. Their gaze caught and the waiter smiled politely, not knowing what was churning beneath Cliff's expressionless composure.

The décor in the Strol restaurant branch in the city of Manchester was samey to those in London. Allen and Walter were sitting opposite to each other on the long large table. Remmick arrived alone and later took his seat at the other end of the same table. Allen and Walter ate their meal in silence in a consumed concentration. Remmick took a swig of the table wine, a wine whose taste and flavour was tailored to the taste of the upper class clients of the Strol chain of restaurant. He let out a loud long belch as he placed the glass noisily on the table. Allen grabbed his half-full wine glass and threw it at Remmick. He pulled the thick white tablecloth up and forward, sending the plates, cups, buckets of ice flying and smashing on the floor and Remmick rushed toward him, and a fight ensued. Fists were flying, the waiters were too stunned to act or approach and separate them. Most of the clients upped and rushed for the exit.

Allen picked a bottle of wine and hit it hard on the red marbled pillar that towered into the lofty ceiling of the restaurant, breaking it into a sharp pointed weapon. He dashed towards Remmick who ran across the room in defence while Allen chased after him. Walter ran after Allen and held him on the hand clutching the weapon and they struggled.

Remmick looked back and on seeing the struggle, he turned towards them and kicked Allen in the stomach and landed him a blow on the jaw. Allen groaned and threw up, he released the weapon he was clutching and slumped sidelong onto the floor. The Strol restaurant security men rushed into the hall and arrested the three. It was quite a scene.

CHAPTER 41
Fulham, London

Field man ten answered the phone on the second ring.

"Hello?" he said calmly into the mouthpiece.

"Your man is somewhere in the centre of Fulham.

"Get it?"

"Keep in touch," said the man in the MI5 office.

"Yes, thanks," responded field man ten and hung up. He turned the key in the ignition switch, engaged the floor gear and nudged the car into traffic on their way to Fulham.

Cliff ate the lunch half way and beckoned to the waiter. He wasn't really hungry and was only able to eat it at all because it was such a delicious meal, especially the melt in the mouth shark flesh. He was tempted to sit tight and wolf down every piece of the dish but he had to make hast because he was there on business, lest he foil his mission. He took out a cigarette, lit it and took a long drag, inhaled and let out a thick plume of smoke.

"The bill, please," he said to the waiter. The waiter turned away and came back with the bill minutes later.

Clifford put £400 in £50 notes in the saucer, stubbed out his half-smoked cigarette in the ash pot, upped and made for the exit door. The waiter turned and watched him leave. He'd not seen anybody pay cash in his eight months in the restaurant.

Field man ten turned the car off the road and parked on the hard shoulder. He put a call through to the MI5 office of the Scotland Yard.

"We are in the centre of Fulham," he said when the call was answered.

"Then call him again," came the reply from the office.

"We will locate him with five metres of error," he added, and hung up.

"Give him a call," said field man ten to his companion. The lady opened the door and stepped down the car and walked the seven metres length to a roadside phone booth. She dialled the number and waited.

"The cell phone you are calling is switched off," came the recorded message.

She went back to the car.

"The phone is switched off," she said.

"Let's give him some ten minutes," replied field man ten.

Cliff was speeding across the Knight's bridge now. He knew that from the Knight's bridge the receptors will receive waves simultaneously. He reached the glove compartment of the car and brought out the mobile phone and pecked the combination digits.

"Pooh! Pooh!! Poooh!!!" hummed the phone then went mute for some ten seconds. Then came the explosions.

"Booom!!! Booooommm!!!!! Booooooommm!!!!!!"

Cliff smiled and switched off the phone and flung it through the car window across the rails of the bridge. The handset tumbled down the several metre height of the bridge before splashing into the river below and sunk deep to the bottom of the slow flowing river.

Field man ten and his companion heard the explosion and minutes later the wailing siren of the police rescue crew. They drove towards the direction of the explosion. The fourth floor of the six-storey building was damaged. As the police rescue crew went into action, the field man and his companion made a call to their office.

"There is an explosion here in the centre of Fulham."

"Your man might be the author. What do you say?"

"Most probably," replied field man ten.

"Keep watch and in touch, we will take precautions," said the man at the office and hung.

Within minutes, roadblocks were mounted on all the roads leading out of Fulham. Cars were stopped and searched but no arrests were made.

Cliff was in his house listening to the news of the bomb explosion on the TV.

"Nobody died but people were seriously wounded but run no risk of life in the hospital where they are being attended to.

"The buildings were seriously damaged and no group has claimed responsibility for the explosions. There is yet another embarrassing fisting in yet another branch of the Strol Restaurant in Manchester," said the reporter.

A smile of pride and satisfaction creased Cliff's face.

"All went as planned," he murmured.

Allen had telephoned him. They had a bail and were released, and they would be coming back to London that night.

CHAPTER 42

The Strol restaurant chain announced a temporary closedown for renovations. It will be another four months before they can open their doors again to the public. The police retrieved the videotapes of the closed circuit system in the three restaurants. They saw the dark-suited blond only in the Oxford Street branch of the restaurant, where he was seated at the far end of the restaurant. The auburn-haired suited gentleman was seen in the Chelsea branch tape, and the silver sprinkled haired don also lunched at a back table of the Fulham branch of the restaurant. The three suited men all arrived alone, brandishing the same type of rich black leather briefcase, and paid their bills with cash. The three bombs all exploded at the back end of the restaurant, and each of the dark suited men opened their briefcases minutes after ordering their meals, glancing discreetly around. But none was seen bringing out or dropping any parcel, because the flap covers of their briefcases were well positioned against the view of the camera. They all ate their lunch half way. All this was no evidence for an indictment, though. Besides, how could they be located? They had all paid cash. Credit cards and cheques would have facilitated things for the investigators. The police watched and rewatched the tapes, but with little success to a clue. None of the dark-suited men touched the tables. And the seats were pulled for them by the waiters on all of the occasions. The plates and the cutlery they used would all have been washed and dried. The Fulham tape was the last the Scotland Yard officers and investigators watched for the day, the tenth time they had watched it in two and a half months. As the tape and the fleeting images wound to the point where the bomb exploded, the twelve-man crew of investigators glanced at one another quizzically.

"Anybody have any idea today?" asked the police captain in charge of the investigations.

"If we could pick the half smoked cigarette," said

one of the investigators.

"A fantastic idea," said the captain. "And he is the only person who'd smoked in the hall that afternoon," he added.

"How can that help the investigations?" asked one of the investigators.

The captain turned and glared at him in disbelief. "The saliva stain on it. A DNA test on it may show if it matches with that of any known criminal. A remote chance, but a chance nonetheless. It's the only lead we have. Do you understand?" said the captain.

The investigator nodded his yes.

A search crew was sent to the Fulham ruins to search for the cigarette butt. It had been almost three months since the bombs exploded and the Strol restaurant share price had fallen from £100 to £30 per share.

At four months after the bomb explosions and closure of the Strol chain of restaurants, they reopened their doors again to the public. Field man ten saw a blond walk into the restaurant and take his seat in the centre of the hall and order a meal and a bottle of wine. The blond looked around and saw people dropping envelopes into the large suggestion box as they left. He smiled an inward smile of praise.

"My intuition has never failed me," he thought. After eating, he scribbled a few words on the paper provided to him by the waiter and looked around to see who was watching him. The field man was busy speaking with the waiter. The blond haired man crouched forward closer to the table and reached the inner pocket of his blazer and brought out a sealed envelope laden with a bomb. He tucked it into the envelope given to him by the waiter and then put the piece of paper inside it. He got up and walked to the suggestion box and pushed the envelope inside it through the opening, and moved on to the Gents. He turned the faucet on and washed his hands. The water was warm and smelled lightly of minerals. He looked himself up in the mirror and ran his fingers backwards through the blond wig and turned to leave.

The field man crossed the doorway into the Gents, and angled his head downwards as the blond gentleman looked at him, avoiding his gaze. But the blond gentleman had seen him fully and there was no mistaking. This was the man who arrested him almost sixteen and a half years ago and arraigned him before the Crown.

"For how long has he been following me, and recording my activities? Probably since I was released from prison, trailing me patiently, never in a hurry, waiting for me to make a mistake. But could he have recognized me in my disguise? Can't really know," thought Cliff.

When the field man came out from the Gents, the blond haired man was nowhere to be seen in the restaurant. He had paid his bill and left.

The bomb exploded forty-five minutes after the blond haired man left the restaurant. He'd detonated the bomb with the same cell phone system he used in the first attacks. It wasn't a very big explosion and nobody died, but the restaurant was destroyed. The Strol restaurant price crashed to a single digit share price of £2.

Mr. Adams announced his resignation to take blame for the security lapses. Tom Tobby made his millions in the put options he bought, about £65 million in profits.

The police and MI5 forensic departments matched the DNA on the saliva-stained half-smoked cigarette obtained from the ruins of the Fulham branch of the Strol restaurant to that of Clifford Dogood, a known terrorist to Scotland Yard.

Chapter 43
Ethiopia
February 2000

A day had never begun better for Gabriel than this morning. He's received a phone call from Tom Tobby, their tickets have been confirmed for tonight to Addis Abbaba, Ethiopia. He, Tom, and Bradley will be travelling together.

He's going home to Addis Abbaba, to his Juba village to pay an old family debt to the Juba god and redeem his family name amongst the Juba folks and be accepted back into his clan as a free kinsman.

The plane touched the Ethiopian soil at 5:30 a.m. Gabriel breathed the arid air of Addis Abbaba, arid though but home air nonetheless. Tom perceived poverty and starvation in the air but never bothered much;

he's here in Addis Abbaba to make his mark in the biotech industry. People will soon be buying stocks in his
company.

Change was slow in the village, and AIDS was still
prevalent. There was no sign of life in Gabriel's family
in the Juba village. Their small hut had fallen and dry
grasses covered the whole compound. The Juba shrine
priest had grown very old and didn't recognize Bradley,
but remembered that some western bioprowlers had
approached him in the fifties to collect some samples
from the Juba shrine. It was a distant memory and so
much has changed. The earth was dry and scorched.
There had been no rain in ten years and the people now
look more ill fed and famished. Life expectancy has
fallen twenty years below what it used to be in the fifties when Bradley visited the Ethiopian country and the
Juba village. The Juba god accepted their burnt offerings and sacrifices, and Gabriel was reaccepted into the
Juba clan as a free kinsman after a lengthy ritual in the
Juba shrine. The patent offices in Addis Abbaba agreed
to give Bradley and Tom a patent for the chemical in the
gut of the Juba frog and for the finished product, but
only if the company will be located and the drug be pro-

duced on Ethiopian soil. Bradley and Tom obliged.

The company, Tom-Gabriel Juba Company Limited, was built opposite the Juba shrine.

At the inauguration ceremony of the company, as Gabriel and Tom posed with the scissors to cut the ribbon, there across the road in front of the Juba shrine was Lazarus, his father, smiling broadly.

"I told you that he'd be back one day. Remember?"

"Yes, I remember, dad," mumbled Gabriel giddily, and Lazarus thinned into the mystic air of the Juba shrine.

Gabriel looked across the faces of the inaugurates and wondered if anybody had heard him speaking with his father's ghost, but nobody showed any surprise or sign. They cut the ribbon and a loud applause ensued.

Bradley smiled heartfully.

"The English and European public health will get better soon. Thank God," he murmured.

Tom looked skywards, the heavy grey cloud was hovering very low, ready to burst and empty its contents. Seconds later, it started to rain.

Clifford was arrested in his house in London and hauled to jail, but he never incriminated Tom Tobby.

Tom deposited £4 million in his savings account and hired him the best lawyer in Britain.

CHAPTER 44

Mr. Clifford Dogood angled his head to look at his defence attorney, Barrister Henry Clark, as he rose to address the court, launching a scathing attack on the prosecuting attorney's submission, citing it as built on distortion and prejudice.

Barrister James, the prosecuting attorney representing the Strol restaurant chain, had denigrated Clifford as a degenerate criminal and terrorist and ridiculed his relatively lavish lifestyle for a person who had just left prison. In his submission, Barrister James devoured Clifford Dogood like a hungry lion would an unfortunate antelope.

"The prosecution have no singular evidence against the accused other than a questionable DNA test match of a saliva-stained cigarette butt that was dubiously found at the site of explosion, three months after the explosion. And because Mr. Clifford Dogood is an ex-convict for bomb blasts, the prosecution makes his case against him. But neither I, nor anybody in this courtroom had ever known the British courts and jury to be unjust. The British court and jury is a just court and hopefully will forever be held as such because we have a crystal and high 'evidence and prove standard'," began Barrister Henry Clark in his upper class London accent.

"The prosecution ridiculed the accused for being an ex-convict and, to the prosecution, ex-convicts must not live a good life. Even in the present century there are still people who prefer toughness to effectiveness in our correctional institutions. While intelligent and progressive minds all around the globe are clamouring for the revisitation of the social engineering of imprisoning people in order to recuperate them, to find a better, more humane way of recuperating delinquents, my honourable legal colleague is pleading to have an innocent man thrown behind bars for life.

Mr. Clifford Dogood as we all know had won lots of kudos serving his army, the IRA . . ."

Cliff's mind skipped. "What is he saying," he

thought.

"He was caught by our elite anti-bomb and anti-terrorism squad, tried and was found guilty and thrown into jail, one of the best correctional institutions on this island. Where he spent the better quarter of the time he has lived on this planet. When he came out of prison, he never rejoined the IRA, or the newer and more violent army – the continuity IRA, which would have befitted a degenerate terrorist. This fact has been attested to by our well-respected police department, the MI5 and Scotland Yard. This act of distancing himself from the IRA, is it an act of a degenerate terrorist as adduced by the prosecution?" he said, going round the jury.

"To my understanding, and I very much believe that to be your understanding also, it means Mr. Clifford Dogood is really rehabilitated and has abhorred all acts of terrorism," continued Barrister Henry Clark, moving his eyes to each member of the twelve-man jury.

"Finding Mr. Clifford Dogood guilty based on his past will be ridiculing our correctional institution and the justice system. Mr. Clifford Dogood needs your vote, yours, yours and yours to be free from the biased net of this unfounded accusation," orated Barrister Henry

Clark, moving his fingers from one juror to the other. He sat down quietly when he'd finished.

After hearing the Judge's summing up, the jury retired to a room to decide their verdict. When they came back to the courtroom, it was a unanimous "not guilty" verdict.

Tom turned in his seat and looked in Mr. Adam's direction, and as their gaze met, he raised his middle finger in a "fuck you" sign and stuck out his tongue at him, and smiled mockingly.

He won at last.

Tom followed Barrister James as he left the courtroom, walking up to him as he descended the court steps.

"Sad to lose, eh? But only good lawyers win headline-grabbing cases. Try to be a good lawyer, it pays," he said to James.

On the steps, at the other side, Mr. Henry Clark, the bespectacled 1.8m tall celebrity lawyer, was besieged by reporters. It was the moment he likes most whenever he wins a high profile case.

"How do you feel sending a criminal, a terrorist, a potential danger, back to the streets to launch new of-

fensives and terrorize the innocent people of Britain?"
asked a reporter.

Henry Clark turned to look at the reporter who asked
the question.

"First of all," he began as camera flashes exploded
in his face, "there is no criminal, no terrorist, no potential danger to the society and there will be no new
offensives from the innocent man. He whom the law
has declared innocent you dare not call a criminal. It
is slander. And I'd rather you withdraw that statement,
otherwise you might be stretching out to grab me before
Clifford Dogood grabs me first and wins the libel suit
that might ensue," warned Henry Clark.

"Secondly, law is a game, a written legal game. And
the thrill of the game is in winning. As a competitor, I
played to win and I won. I'm a lawyer and as a lawyer I
defend the innocent from persecution and protect the
guilty against vengeance. I love the part I play. I have no
regrets. After all, who is all that innocent, righteous or
guilty? Well, at least not the prosecutor, the Judge, the
jury, nor the society at large.

"Get the drift?" he orated amidst more explosions of
camera flashes.

About the Author

Obi Orakwue is a Biochemist and Research Associate.
Presently he's busy pruning his latest work entitled
"Career Spouse".

His other works include:

Fiction
- Overqualified Labourer
- The Terrorist Creed
- Comedy of Time
- The Lost Gene
- Victim of Want

Non-fiction
- A Complete Guide to Overcome 'No Canadian
  Experience': How and Where to Obtain
  'Canadian Experience'
- Two-Dozen Businesses You Can Start and Run in
  Canada, The USA and Elsewhere
- Immigrate, Live, Work, Study and do Business
  in Canada

He lives in Toronto, Canada.